SCENE THROUGH A REARVIEW MIRROR

A Backward Glance

JIM SHIELDS

This is a work of fiction. All of the characters, names, incidents, organizations, and dialogue in this novel are either the products of the author's imagination or are used fictitiously.

ISBN: 978-1-6847-0454-5 (sc)
ISBN: 978-1-6847-0453-8 (e)

Library of Congress Control Number: 2019907142

Lulu Publishing Services rev. date: 07/09/2019

With gratitude to all who made this book come to life;

And so may a slow
wind work these words
of love around you,
an invisible cloak
to mind your life.

Beannacht John O'Donoghue

Contents

Through a Rearview Mirror

He went to the library to search for anything he could find on Japan in preparation for a surprise holiday he was planning for his wife. Anything on Tokyo and Kyoto that would reveal the contrasts and tensions between tradition and modernity that characterize Japan today would suffice. This surprise holiday would be his wife's first time in Japan, and he wanted her to enjoy the experience to the fullest.

A short search unearthed what he was looking for in the travel section. He made his selections, browsed biographies, passed the time of day with a few acquaintances, checked out his books using the newly installed automatic checkout machine—ACM—with help from a librarian, and headed for his car in the adjacent car park.

It was a beautiful sunny afternoon. Groundsmen were busy at their work, mowing and trimming with characteristic languor, saturating the still air with the strong smell of freshly cut grass that, for some reason unknown to him, reminded him of cats.

Exiting the car park, he turned left onto the main road, busy with traffic. It was that time of day when schools emptied the nation's future to waiting buses and queues of parent-piloted vehicles mustered expectantly. The traffic lights controlling the T junction fifty meters in front of him conveniently turned green, permitting him to proceed straight through. Two hundred meters farther, another set of traffic lights at the top of a short incline controlled a T junction and pedestrian crossings. The stem of this T junction joined the main road from his left a few meters beyond the pedestrian crossing. It was always busy with vehicles and pedestrians.

Approaching this set of traffic lights behind a string of slow-moving traffic, he noticed a police car and a paramedic mobile unit among other vehicles parked outside a battery of fast-food outlets on his right. The traffic lights were showing green; he was good to go. *Must be my lucky day,* he thought.

About one hundred meters through the junction, he spotted two boys on his passenger side, running pell-mell on the pavement toward the intersection. The leading boy looked to be about twelve years old. His blond hair flopped up and down as he raced his companion with the energy possessed only by the young.

Captivated by their youthful exuberance, he kept a glancing eye on them through his rearview mirror. One eye on the road, the other eye on the boys still racing each other, the blond boy now led by about ten meters, and the traffic light ahead of him still showed green. Instantly in his gut, he knew that the boy would mistake the green traffic light for the pedestrian crossing signal and dart across the road, oblivious to danger. He watched transfixed, certain of what was going to happen, knowing there was nothing he could do to prevent it other than hope and pray that something, someone, somehow would deflect the boy racer.

As all this was going through his mind, a bus passed him on his right, heading toward the junction. In his rearview mirror, he watched, transfixed, as the blond boy grasped the traffic light column, swung around it twice to gain momentum, and propelled himself across the road into the path of the oncoming bus. The huge front wheel crushed the boy's head like a watermelon; death was instantaneous. In slow motion, it seemed the bus stuttered apologetically to a halt, straddling the pedestrian crossing, its engine groaning and the remains of the squashed boy spread on the tarmac surface beneath it.

Stunned, riveted, shocked, disbelieving, he almost rammed the back of the truck in front of him. He pulled over, parked, and sprinted back toward the mayhem erupting back down the road. Police and paramedics at the fast-food outlets he had passed, alerted by the commotion, were already on the scene when he got there. It was clear that there was nothing anyone could do for the boy; he knew that already from what he had seen in his rearview mirror. The other boy was being attended to by the paramedics; he was in shock, as was the bus driver. There was nothing she could have done. He wanted to tell her that, but she was surrounded by people. More onlookers gathered. There was nothing he could do that wasn't already being done. He felt he was only in the way, impotently gawking, and he left the scene traumatized and drove home. On the short journey home, the rearview mirror scene replayed in slow motion over in his mind like an old black-and-white movie. He somehow knew it was going to happen, saw it happen, and could do absolutely nothing to prevent it. *Premonition, intuition—call it what you will*, he thought as he recalled his mother often saying, "I knew that was going to happen." But on this occasion, he was absolutely certain about what was going to happen, and it did.

From home, he reported the accident to the police, told them what he had witnessed and that their colleagues were already on the scene. Then he sat down, wept uncontrollably, and told his wife everything—that somehow he knew it was going to happen and how he could do nothing to prevent it. She listened, made coffee, listened again as, distraught and in search of explanations, he repeated what he had just witnessed. When he had talked himself out, she put her arms around him and held him close. How long they sat in each other's embrace he didn't know. His thoughts had turned to the boy's parents, the bus driver, and the person who would knock on the parents' door to tell them that their child had been killed crossing the road at a pedestrian crossing. The parents would want to know every detail, every awful, minute detail. They would insist; they needed to know; they would want to see him. As he lay in his coffin, his mother would want to touch him, touch his cheek, kiss his brow, hold his hand to say goodbye. He could tell them everything; he saw it happen in slow motion. But he couldn't, and he wouldn't; they had enough loss and hurt to bear as it was, and he wasn't going to add to it. The very thought of the horror he had witnessed made him screw his eyes tightly shut, tighten every muscle in his body, curl his fingers and toes until he was rigid from head to toe with an intensity so unbearable he had to force his mind to shut down. He knew that the death of a child is one of the few things—perhaps the only thing—parents could not believe.

He knew the bus driver, blameless as she was, in her anguish would find ways to fault herself. She would need professional help dealing with that. Nothing he could do there. He wasn't asked for a witness statement by the police; they didn't need it, with plenty of other witnesses.

He didn't go the funeral, not because he didn't want to but because he just couldn't bear it. Words he had heard read at funerals filled his mind. They appeared to die; their going felt like a disaster, their leaving like annihilation. What he had witnessed was more than annihilation; it was obliteration. He felt for the parents, standing graveside as they heard the dull, hollow sounds of the first shovelfuls of earth landing on the coffin lid.

For weeks after the accident, he avoided the area, taking alternative routes, bypassing it. As time passed, he knew he would have to overcome his reluctance to visit the scene; avoidance was not the answer. He chose a Sunday morning when the junction was quiet with traffic. He drove through it as he had that fateful day, parked where he had parked before, and retraced his steps to the pedestrian crossing where he had witnessed the boy being killed—squashed like a bug. He walked slowly across the pedestrian crossing. There was a dark, sand-encrusted stain on the road, a gritty smear left by workmen cleaning up the mess of a boy's death. It was the only tangible sign that something dreadful had happened there a few short weeks earlier. Vehicles passed over it, and pedestrians trod on it oblivious; everyday life carried on. Normal service had resumed. But a boy's life had been tragically, brutally extinguished there. His parents would never be the same. Nor would his friend or the bus driver. Nor would he. Their futures had all been cruelly reshaped one way and another. But he wasn't thinking about that then; that thought would surface later. He saw again the wheel of the bus crush the life from the boy, shuddering as the black-and-white images flashed through his mind.

A couple of weeks later, the flashbacks started. In his sleep, everything from the moment he left the library until he got home that afternoon played in his mind over and over again in slow motion, until he would wake in a cold sweat, shaking. It was his Groundhog Day afternoon. At home in the garden, mowing the lawn, the smell of freshly cut grass would bring it all flooding back, and he would have to pause what he was doing.

It had happened a long time ago on a beautiful sunny late afternoon on his way home from the library as witnessed through his rearview mirror. The flashbacks were less frequent, but the incident was forever chiseled into his mind. In the decades that had slipped past, he had come to understand that there was a huge chasm between feeling others' pain and bearing it. It was time to let go and let living work its healing miracle.

Wee Daft Dicky

He was christened Richard, but his pals called him by his familiar name, "Wee Dicky." Stretching to his full height of four feet nine in his football shoes with the longest cleats in, the "Wee" perfectly described his stature. The daft was added later, after a series of unfortunate escapades. Two of the foolish things, among others, that earned Wee Dicky his full title involved a freezer and cheese.

A widow woman was living on her own down a lane round the corner from where Dicky lived in a neat little row of six small kitchen houses. A friend had offered her for the taking away a fridge freezer that she was replacing. The widow thought at last she could rid herself of the meat safe that hung outside on her yard wall attracting flies; she was made up. Her only problem was that she had no way of getting the fridge freezer from her friend's house to hers. Up stepped Wee Dicky when he heard of her plight and offered to do the job free—gratis. So off he went to pick up the fridge freezer in his Ford Fiesta. He had to get help from lads on the street corner to lift the fridge freezer onto the roof of the Fiesta, ignoring suggestions that he would be better off with a roof rack. He secured the fridge freezer on the roof by looping ropes over it and passing them through the front and rear windows of the Fiesta, tying them in knots he had learned in the scouts. He wasn't daft though; he knew his precarious load would if spotted attract the attention of the local constabulary, so he transported the fridge freezer under cover of darkness. It was not an easy journey; the wind had got up, and the Fiesta was like a rudderless boat in a heavy swell, and it barely made it up the hill to the widow's house. But with perseverance he got it there.

Again Wee Dicky cast around for help and eventually press-ganged a couple of pals to help him unload the fridge freezer and maneuver it to the widow's front door. That's when the revelation came that the door was too narrow for the passage of the fridge freezer. It was dark and getting late, so Wee Dicky parked the fridge freezer in the lane at the widow's door with assurance he would be back in the morning without fail to finish the job. Overnight it rained.

Next morning, Wee Dicky heading for the widow's house spotted birds splashing in water on the roof of his Fiesta. That's when he discovered the huge dent in the roof made when transporting the fridge freezer the night before. But fair play to Wee Dicky, he just took it in his stride and sallied forth to get the fridge freezer into the widow's house.

Well, he tried it this way and that way; he scratched his head a time or two, but all he ended up with was an itchy scalp. Whichever way he looked to maneuver it, the fridge freezer through the door would not go. He considered taking the door off its hinges and removing the door frame, but that wouldn't work either. He was despondent to the point of giving up when he remembered once seeing a coffin being taken out through a front room window of a house farther down the lane because the geometry of the vestibule made it impossible for it to be removed with dignity.

That's it, thought Wee Dicky, *we'll manage the fridge freezer in through the window.* But he wasn't daft. He measured everything twice and jotted all the measurements down with the stub of a pencil on the back of a fag packet to be sure his brainwave would work before he set about removing the window. Eventually, window removed with help from neighbors, he got the fridge freezer through the window safely into the widow's front room. *Job done*, he thought.

The day was changing; rain was imminent. Wee Dicky's priority now was to reinstall the window to make the widow's house weathertight. He had just finished when the heavens opened, and rain came down like stair rods bouncing off the surface of the lane. *Thank God I got that window in*,

Wee Dicky thought. Feeling satisfied with his efforts, Wee Dicky asked the widow where she would like him to put the fridge freezer. "Auch, just bring it through into the scullery. I've made room for it," she said. That's when the penny dropped like a brick onto Wee Dicky's foot. The inside door was narrower than the outside door; if that wasn't bad enough, there was another narrow opening to negotiate to get into the scullery There was no way short of knocking walls down to get the fridge freezer into the widow's scullery. Well, you've heard the saying never pour water on a drowned mouse. Wee Dicky wasn't drowned; he was crushed.

But though crushed, if nothing else he was pragmatic; he knew, as they say, that there's no use looking for the ladle when the pot's on fire. So to cut a long story short, after some persuading he convinced the widow that the fridge freezer won't look out of place in her front room and that the arrangement would give her more useful space in her scullery. Today the fridge freezer proudly sits in the widow's front room in a recess beside the fireplace topped with a potted aspidistra and adorned with strategically placed magnetically fixed framed photos of her children, grandchildren, and great-grandchildren. From the wall opposite the fridge freezer a framed picture of the Sacred Heart of Jesus offered the widow comfort.

The removal of the meat safe from the widow's whitewashed yard wall left a bare patch. Wee Dicky, generous to a fault, offered to whitewash the whole yard for the widow.

She graciously declined his offer.

Sometime after the fridge freezer incident, a house fire occurred up the road from where Wee Dicky lived. Fortunately there was no life loss or serious injury, but the family that lived there lost everything and had to be temporarily rehoused. The community rallied around to help the family. Wee Dicky, unsolicited, volunteered to organize a fund-raising event, which he did. He came up with the idea of a cheese-rolling competition down Hunter's field based on Easter egg rolling that occurred there every year on Easter Day. Children would go out and harvest the blossom on whin bushes; hen's eggs would be hardboiled in whin-blossom-infused water, giving the eggs a range of bright yellow hues. The colors of the eggs could be changed depending on what dyes were added to the water. Egg rolling on Easter day was always great fun.

For the cheese rolling event, Wee Dicky negotiated a deal with the local cheese maker to produce three-pound cheese rolls at cost for competitors to purchase at an agreed reasonable markup, with all the profits made going to aid the fire-impoverished family.

Hunter's field had about a one-in-ten gradient. It was fairly steep and stretched roughly 150 yards from the top to the bottom bounded by a fence consisting of little more than a couple of strands of wire. Beyond the fence in close proximity ran the narrow-gauge railway line.

A date was fixed for the cheese-rolling competition, and publicity flyers were distributed. Needless to say, the cheddar cheese rolls sold like hotcakes. To ensure fairness, Wee Dicky arranged for several wooden chutes to be made similar to the roll a penny holders used at carnival amusements to allow several cheeses to be rolled at the same time and also to ensure that all the cheeses were released in a similar fashion. Willie if nothing else was fair-minded and thorough. Prizes would be awarded to the three cheeses that reached the fence at the bottom of the hill in the shortest time.

The competition started on schedule and was progressing very well; everyone was having a great time. It was a hot summer day, and the people were enjoying themselves; the refreshments stands were doing great business, and everyone was in high spirits one way and another.

Occasionally passenger trains passed along the narrow-gauge railway at the bottom of Hunter's field. As the day progressed, cheese rolls pierced the permeable fence, getting onto the railway track. The wheels of passing passenger trains at first easily shredded the cheese rolls that got onto the rails, but as the rails were gradually smeared with a cheesy scum, the trains started to encounter some difficulties. The wheels of the engines pulling the trains started spinning and losing traction, but they still managed to make it over that part of the cheese-contaminated track. Later in the afternoon, a train of coal wagons arrived on the scene. Heavily laden, it only managed to get a short distance along the cheese-scum-coated rails. The engine pulling the coal train chugged and chugged and slithered and slathered until its wheels, spinning with increased velocity, lost traction completely, and the train started sliding slowly backward.

To the crowd enjoying the cheese-rolling competition, the back-sliding train was just added value; they hooted, cheered, and laughed until it slowly disappeared back the way it had come round the bend in the track out of sight. They were blissfully unaware of the possibility of a collision with another upcoming train. Thankfully, however, the coal train was safely brought to a halt, and immediate danger was averted.

The cheese-rolling competition continued unabated until the local constabulary intervened and summarily brought it to a halt. Then the fire brigade appeared and busied itself trying to cleanse the railway track of the offending greasy cheese scum.

Wee Dicky, identified as the organizer of the event, was escorted to the police station for questioning with the possibility of charges looming. In the end, when the purpose of the cheese-rolling competition was realized and that a lot of money had been raised for the impoverished family, the threat of charges subsided, and Wee Dicky was released with a severe warning.

In the pub one night, his pals were having a good laugh about the cheese-rolling escapade when someone remarked, "See, Wee Dicky he's as daft as a brush," to which someone else responded, "That's right enough, Wee Daft Dicky."

From that night, Wee Dicky ever after was known as Wee Daft Dicky.

No one ever claimed to have uttered the phrase Wee Daft Dicky, not that it matters now. But that didn't stop Wee Daft Dicky from doing other daft things, but that's a story for another day.

You know, to this day folk still talk about that cheese-rolling competition.

A Cold Caller

Their morning coffee was interrupted by a hesitant knocking on their front door. Fred asked his wife, Nora, "Are we expecting anyone?"

"Not that I know of," Nora responded.

Placing his coffee cup carefully on the doily protecting the coffee table—Nora was fussy about things like that—Fred eased himself out of his comfortable chair and went to silence the offending door. Opening it, he found himself looking down at a woman standing on the path, looking up at him. She was neatly dressed; her coal black hair touched her shoulders, and two velvety brown eyes smiled cheerfully at him out of a ruddy lived-in-looking face. A black leather shoulder bag hung by her side. Her only adornment was a pair of small stud diamond ear rings. "I'm sorry to trouble you," she said, "but I wonder if you could help me."

Fred, caught slightly off balance by her directness, muttered, "I don't really know if I can!"

"Oh, it's just that I'm a Catholic and my husband's a Protestant," she volunteered by way of explanation.

"But what's that got to do with me?" Fred said, confusion crossing his face like a fleeting black cloud polluting a blue sky.

"Haven't you something to do with that Protestant church up there?" she said, pointing a finger toward the top of the town.

"Yes, I have," Fred answered, stretching out the *yessss*, wondering what on earth could be coming next. "I'm a board member."

Then Nora, her curiosity getting the better of her, called out, "Who's at the door, Fred?"

"It's a Catholic woman, Nora, with a Protestant husband looking for help," Fred answered, not realizing what he was actually saying and how ridiculous it sounded. The woman in front of him was wearing walking shoes; she wasn't tall, but she wasn't petite either. There was something appealing about her, other than her immediate need; she seemed open, uncomplicated, and genuine.

Nora, appearing at Fred's side, quickly sized up the situation and invited their cold caller in. Settled in the lounge with a cup of coffee, the woman proceeded to introduce herself and explain why she unannounced had presented herself at their front door. "My name is Francis Ferguson. I live in Black's Lane. I'm a Roman Catholic," she said, laughing, "but I don't roam anywhere much, if going to chapel isn't counted as roaming. You see," she continued, "my husband, Max, is a Protestant, and I'm worried about him; you know, if anything happens to me, he doesn't go anywhere, if you know what I mean, and I'd like to try and ready him, prepare him for, you know. So I'm trying to get him together with his own folk, like, you know what I mean, and somebody told me that you had something to do with the Protestant church over the wall from us." The wall she was referring to was a six-foot-high basalt stone boundary wall between Black's Lane and the church domain.

Fred confirmed that he was indeed a board member of the Presbyterian Church "over the wall" from Black's Lane, as she had described it. "How do you join?" she asked. "That's very easy," Fred replied. "In fact, you completed the first step by letting me know that you want Max to join our congregation. The next step in the process is to pledge a donation to the operating fund of the church." He effortlessly produced from the bureau beside him, like a magician pulling a rabbit out of a hat, a box of weekly donation envelopes. Placing the box of envelopes on the coffee table in front of Francis, he said, "All you have to do is put a little"—emphasizing the *little* lest he frightened her off—"something in an envelope each week. That's the next step. Then he will have to attend an orientation session and volunteer for at least one activity, and that's it; he's in—a member of our congregation."

"It's as easy as that?" she asked, somewhat surprised.

"It's as easy as that, simple," Fred assured her.

The woman hesitated, uncertain and somewhat bemused. Fred thought he had frightened her off, but she raised her head, looked him straight in the eye seeking further assurance, and inquired, "He doesn't have to do any courses or anything—no schooling in what he's supposed to be protesting about or anything like that, or what he's supposed to believe in?"

"No," Fred assured her.

"You see, in our church it's not that easy; there's all sorts of things to do before you're let in, proper that is," she volunteered, seeking reassurance.

Fred said, "It's that easy, believe me."

"About the protesting, he can't walk too far with his arthritis, you know. Is that all right?" she said.

Fred's face opened in a smile like sunshine on a summer's day, and laughing, he said, "We don't do the protesting thing anymore; that's all long gone. We're a bit more civilized now."

Satisfied, Francis picked up the box, slipped out an envelope, wrote her husband's name on it, took a purse out of her shoulder bag, found some coins, put them in the envelope, and left it unsealed on the coffee table.

With Max's admission into the welcoming fold of Presbyterianism settled, Nora cleared the tea things away; they chatted for a while before parting as friends on first name terms. On her way out, she was given the obligatory tour around Fred's garden—his pride and joy. At the garden gate Francis, patting the bag carelessly slung over her shoulder, asked, "What about the other envelopes, then?"

"Auch, no bother. Sure you're only a stone's throw from here, so I'll call and collect them," Fred offered.

With that, Francis went on her way up the road light in heart, a spring in her step. He watched her go until a bend in the road took her out of his line of sight. Unbeknown to them that morning, a lifelong friendship was conceived—a friendship that would blossom and deepen with time.

Fred would be like a rent collector on a Friday night; he would call with Francis to collect the weekly church donation. He recalled the first time, knocking on the door of her midterrace house on Black's Lane, thinking that as a church board member he might be exploiting her concern for her husband's spiritual well-being. It was a doorstep examination of conscience, immediately set to rest when Francis, smiling, opened her door to his tentative knock. Ushered into the front room, he was welcomed by the aroma of fresh home-baked breads sitting atop her turf-fired range. The room was small; a chaise longue was set against one wall; a small drop-leaf table and chairs nestled in front of the window overlooking the narrow lane, and a pine dresser fitted neatly into the recess by the side of the range. The top of the dresser was populated by a forest of family snapshots, the shelves underneath filled with shining white and blue and speckled delft. The floor beneath his feet was covered with patterned linoleum. It reminded him of his childhood home; his mother had a chaise longue in her front room, which she often referred to as the fainting couch, though he never found out why. The room had a warm feel about it that wasn't coming just from the range; it had personality. It was welcoming, bright, and cheerful.

While he was lost in thought, Francis lifted the leaf of the table, swung the supporting frame into place beneath it, and arranged a tablecloth neatly on top. Then she sat him down facing the front window, with a mug of strong tea accompanied with warm fresh-baked wheaten bread, generously buttered. Looking out the front window, he could see the roof of the church, over the wall, as Francis had described it. Two hours later, after she insisted he tried her delicious shortbread, he had to drag himself away. Nora would wonder where in God's name he was, and folk might get the wrong idea, not that that bothered him; he was thinking of her.

Then one Friday evening he called looking forward as always to meeting Francis, but on this occasion Francis's husband Max opened the door to his knock. Fred stood rooted to the spot, his mouth silently opening and closing in slow motion like a toad with laryngitis. Max beamed a welcoming, "Hello, Fred, how are you doing? Come on in. Francis told me all about you." Francis, in the middle of sorting the washing she had just brought in from the yard, said, "Auch, sure, it's yourself Fred; sit yourself down, and we'll have a cup of tea." He did as he was bid—knowing she wouldn't take no for an answer—drank the tea and ate all that went with it, and chatted about all sorts of things before taking his leave with the donation envelope pocketed.

As time passed, he got to know both of them very well. They became firm friends. Fred was struck by the simplicity of their way of living. They were completely open to each other and to him; they didn't say one thing and mean another. He was to discover they were this way with everybody; it was just them being themselves. Thanks to them he would often revisit, examine, and refresh his way of living.

Getting to know Francis was in many ways like peeling an onion without the tears. There were days when he laughed himself silly. She was a deep reservoir of stories, folklore, songs seldom sung, and memories of places and people, from which she would regale him to his heart's delight. As their friendship deepened, he realized that Francis was a very knowledgeable woman, not in an academic sense, much more profound than that—knowledgeable about a simple chosen way of living, renewed and refreshed every day. He was later to learn that the bedrock on which her way of life was founded was the beatitudes, as she interpreted them. He came to understand that the term *practicing Catholic* meant to her total commitment; hers was a living faith—care of the neighbor started, reached and spread out from her hearth. It was all embracing, unencumbered, and inclusive.

Slowly Fred became privy to the story of her life. Not the whole story, but the part she would talk freely about. Francis and Max, both in their early twenties, had married and set up home in Black's Lane. Francis worked as a finishing seamstress in the local clothing factory, and Max as a pattern maker in the foundry. They followed their own religious pathways, which at the time might have seemed unusual, incompatible, but for them it was normal. Francis would go to first mass on a Sunday morning to be on hand to make sure that Max was well turned out for his church service later that morning. She knew that in certain traditions appearance was important; folk noticed.

They had two children—a boy and a girl—close together, so that they would be company for each other. The children, Len and Lily, grew up enjoying a freedom, now for many children constrained as communities changed, reshaped, and lost their essence and neighborliness. There was no disagreement about the choice of their children's first school. They went to school with their friends nurturing enduring friendships. Worship was not a problem either; it too was approached in a practical, sensible way. Sometimes the children would go to chapel with their mother and at other times to church with their father. Conventions and attitudes of do-gooders didn't matter to Francis and Max; they lived their lives how they chose to live, unencumbered. They reasoned that in time when their children were old enough, they would choose for themselves the pathways they would take in life. Francis often reminded Max that they were only the builders laying the foundations.

Len and Lily matriculated and then graduated, to their parent's great delight, in medicine and philosophy, respectively. Both married, and true to form, you might say, one in a Catholic church and the other in a Presbyterian church. Lily obtained a postgraduate research position, obtained her doctorate, and was appointed as a university lecturer. Dr. Len Ferguson became a consultant in his chosen field, in the process losing the title doctor to become a mister again. Eminent in his field, he was head hunted to lead a team of researchers at the forefront of cancer research in America. It was the opportunity of a lifetime. The pros and cons of accepting the position and the impact on family—he had three children by this stage—were carefully considered and discussed. In the end the consensus decision was to accept.

As time eased toward their departure, the excitement generated by Len's appointment slowly dissipated, and a coarse blanket of quiet resignation wrapped around Francis and Max. They tried to hide their inner feelings, but separation and distance were heavy in the air they breathed. The unbridgeable expanse of the wild Atlantic Ocean became a sea of separation. It was heartrending for Francis and Max, but they celebrated as best they could with cheerful disposition their family gatherings, with small talk deliberately focused on the positives for everyone and anxieties well concealed.

Suddenly, it seemed they were standing on the station platform, with goodbyes exchanged and hugs and kisses repeated until they forced themselves to part. Len and his family boarded the train on the start of their journey to Southampton, in England, where after an overnight stay they would embark on an ocean liner for America. On time the train departed; they were gone, slowly at first, arms waving until it was pointless waving anymore. Gone from their sight but still Francis and Max stood on the station platform, like pillars of stone, until the black smoke pouring out the steam engine's stack slowly blended into the darkness of the night. Walking home supported by Max, Francis wept. She wept in Max's arms in bed that night too.

Transatlantic communication then was via a cable laid on the seabed; it was by today's technology crude and generally inaccessible. Their social media was the local newspaper; 24-7 communication for them hadn't yet materialized. The internet was just a fermentation crystallizing in somebody's head; information technology had yet to make instant twenty-four-seven communication available worldwide to all. Francis didn't have a telephone or television in her home; neither did anyone else in her neighborhood. Communication by letter post could take at least up to three weeks from posting to arrival at its destination in America, and another three weeks to receive a reply by return. They suffered these periods of information deprivation with characteristic forbearance. In the ten months Len and his family had settled in America, Francis and Max received six letters from them. Everything was great; the job was going well; Len's wife was working in the same hospital; the children's schooling was going well; they were making friends and looking forward to coming home on holiday soon to see them all. All the usual stuff including details of their grandchildren's measles, cut fingers, and bruised toes, filling pages and pages of trivia that Francis and Max eagerly devoured. Francis didn't just read the letters; she scrutinized them for any hint, trace, or tone that might suggest all was not as well as was being portrayed. She found nothing to concern her; thus after due diligence, each letter was placed in the biscuit tin she kept on top of the wardrobe in their bedroom for safekeeping and future reading.

They had decided on having an early night one Friday night to be in good form for the weekend they had planned. At about half past two on Saturday morning they were awakened by urgent banging on their front door. At first, half asleep, they thought they were imagining things; then Francis leaped out of bed, shouldered her dressing gown, and ran down the stairs to silence the door. Max was not far behind her as she swung open the door to find a buttoned black uniform with chevron-marked sleeves filling her eyes and under a peeked cap the face of the local police sergeant, a man she knew well. From the look on his face, the set of his shoulders, and his reluctant eyes, she knew immediately that he was not the bearer of good news. The pit of her stomach swelled with fear; she felt weak at the knees and clung to the door to keep herself upright. Lights were coming on in the neighbors' houses next door. She brought the sergeant in and closed the door behind him; he was uncomfortable, she could sense that; his serious eyes fleetingly engaged with hers. Max pulled out chairs from under the table and sat the sergeant down. Francis hunched forward on the chaise longue, hands clasped, knuckles white between her knees looked like an animal in pain. "Why are you here? What's wrong?"

Slowly the sergeant told them what he knew; information had been received that their son, Len, had been involved in an accident on the freeway near where he worked, on Wednesday past. He was in the hospital, the hospital where he worked, but as yet they had no information as to his condition. "What happened?" Francis asked.

"We don't know," the sergeant answered, "but we're trying to find out as much as we can, as soon as we can."

"Was his wife and children with him? Are they all right; is he badly hurt?" Francis continued, anxiety shaping her face. Many questions later, to which he had no useful answers, the sergeant left them with the assurance he would return when he had more to tell them.

It was a long night without sleep. They sat in silence, anxious, worried, as the early-morning shadows retreated along the brightening lane, inwardly hoping it was all just a bad dream. How long they sat Francis didn't know. It was her next-door neighbors coming round to ask about the carry on last night that forced them from their state of shock, bewilderment, and confusion. That's when Francis realized that they had to let their daughter, Lily, know what had happened. She checked her purse for coinage and hurried to the nearest telephone box. The morning dragged slowly into afternoon with Francis and Max fingertip clinging to hope. Silent pleading prayers petitioned heavenward for Len's well-being. In a mire of uncertainty all day, they waited.

In early evening the sergeant returned to confirm that Len was in the hospital, that his condition was serious, and that everything that could be done for him was being done. Francis bombarded him with questions; How serious? Was he in pain? What about his family? What happened? He told them all he knew; he could tell them no more. Taking his leave, he assured them that all that could be done to find out more was being done. When he had gone, the neighbors called round again to hear the latest news. It was that kind of close knit community—a neighbor's trouble was a shared trouble, bonding them. The evening stretched long into night; word swiftly passed around the neighborhood; friends called to the house, offering support and companionship, and allowing Francis to vent her feelings and fears. Max coped in silence, as men usually do.

On Sunday morning after another night of fitful sleep, they were roused by a blackbird greeting the morning in song from the top of the chestnut tree in the precincts of the church. Angrily Max looked through the bedroom window at the blackbird, thinking, You're lucky; you have something to sing about. But you're all right; fortunately I don't have a gun. Breathing in deeply, his boiling anger slowly dissipated. Sunday passed quickly, with friends and neighbors coming and going, with no further update on Len's condition, but worry and anxiety nibbled at them every minute of the passing day; there was no respite.

It was Monday midmorning when the sergeant returned, accompanied by an inspector. When Francis opened the door and saw the two of them, she knew immediately in her gut that it was the news she had been dreading. She would have fallen on top of them, if Max, close behind her and alert to the possibility, hadn't grabbed her just in time. Inside the house, Francis slowly regained a semblance of composure. Seated, the inspector relayed all that he knew. There was no fault on Len's part; he was a passenger on a bus when a truck collided with it. Len was rushed to the hospital, and they did everything they could, but they couldn't save him. He was alone at the time; his family was not involved. "Thank God for that," Francis responded from the depths of her being. "Did he suffer? What were his injuries? How did it happen? Where was he going? Who was with him? How long did it take for the ambulance to get to him?" She loosed a torrent of questions at him. The inspector recited the bare facts, as he knew them, but it wasn't enough; it could never be enough. Francis wanted to know, needed to know, everything, every minute detail. They talked for a long time as Francis and Max struggled to come to terms with the fact that their son, Len, was dead, tragically killed in a road traffic accident, in the land of the free. When the policemen were about to take their leave, Max, who had been silent since their arrival, simply asked, "What can we do?" The policemen looked at each other; the inspector, taking Max's hand, shook it saying, "We will do everything we can for you," and with that, they left Max and Francis to themselves.

Alone, devastated, they sat in numbed silence; they didn't know what to do and didn't know what they could do; together they sat and wept. When Len had left them standing on the station platform as he departed for America, he said, "Don't be sad; don't be lonely. It's for the best; we'll be back often to see you." Sadness filled their home then, but it was nothing like the sadness—the emotional pain of loss and hopelessness—that gripped their home now. It seeped out into Black's Lane and far beyond like a black bituminous sludge.

Friends and neighbors rallied around them in support, as Francis and Max hovered in a limbo of intense grief, impotence, inadequacy, and helplessness. The things some neighbors said—a child shouldn't die before its parents; time will heal; it's all for the better in the end; he's in a better place; sure it won't be long till we're all with him—sounded so empty and hollow to Francis. Those that knew better kept their mouths shut, made do with a hug, and listened to her, when she had something to say. Emotionally she felt like a caged bird. Angry with God, she screamed, "Why did you let it happen?" All the while Max at her side was manly in his grief. Silent. Alone with Francis remembering his son, he was unmanly—nursed through infancy, nourished through childhood, guided through adolescence, mentored to maturity, given wings to fly, and freed to go solo, wherever his imagination would take him. He was heartbroken.

At some point, she couldn't remember when, Francis went to the phone box and rang Lily to tell her through sobs and tears that Len had been killed in America. Lily, home on compassionate leave, freed her parents from some of the burden of grief. She allowed her mother to treat her as a visitor, making her breakfast, shopping with her, and going to mass, all the while easing Francis back into her routine. Her father she encouraged back to work; he went when he realized there was little else he could do. Lily arranged telephone access so that her parents could talk to Len's wife and children, which they did. Francis did most of the talking. Lily also set up a system for regular contact via the transatlantic telephone system on specific dates and times. She also encouraged her mother back to work. Satisfied that she had done all she could and that her parents were in good shape, it was time for Lily to leave. Tears were shed at her going, but there was a trace of resilience in them too.

As the weeks passed, patience—the hard teacher—quieted their emotions and helped them to focus on what they could best do for Len's family. After much discussion and careful consideration, it was settled that Len's remains be cremated and accompany his family on their return home.

It was almost a year later when, with Len's affairs in America settled, his family returned home. With most of their stuff in storage, they stayed with Francis and Max until they sorted a place of their own. It was a bit cramped; the house was full to overflowing, but they made do, and life went on. Len's remains were interred in the family plot his parents had chosen in the local cemetery a long time ago, never expecting that anyone would occupy it before them. Before it fills up too much, Francis had advised; she was always the one with the farsighted eye, Max was often heard to remark. It was a simple family occasion. Len's name was the first on the headstone. They gladly child-minded their grandchildren when their mother went back to work. She was a doctor too. Life assumed a sort of normality, or so it might have seemed to the casual observer. Len's wife bought a new-build house and moved out with her children, leaving Francis and Max feeling a little bit at a loss. But that feeling was short-lived; they may have moved a little distance away, but in a strange way, as family they moved even closer together.

Francis and Max, though devastated by Len's tragic death, coped in different ways. Max experienced great difficulty with the notion of a loving, caring God. He pondered on the biblical references to the sins of the father, wondering what had he done to deserve such vengeful retribution. It was something in the context of world affairs that had troubled him for a long time, why God allowed such things to happen. He began occasionally missing Sunday service until finally he stopped going altogether. It would be a long time before he could give voice to his feelings, never mind accepting his loss. Francis had the same raw, wounded feelings as Max but somehow, maybe because she was a mother, understood that accidents were a part of life. Random events happened all the time, to other people, below their radar; this time it happened to them. It was their turn in the roulette of life.

As time passed, there were moments of celebration. Their daughter Lily reached the top of her profession, becoming a professor in a prestigious university in England. It was a proud Francis who listened to her daughter's professorial lecture, though she didn't understand much of it, undaunted in the presence of elite academia. Francis, humble in spirit, was at ease in any company.

It was concern for Max's spiritual well-being that had brought Francis to Fred. Fred's visits to their home assumed in a curious way a ministry of encouragement to Max through listening. Eventually, with friendly perseverance, he persuaded Max to accompany him to Sunday service. Once back in the fold, it was not long before Max felt spiritually refreshed enough to go solo again. Francis went to first mass on Sunday, as well as every other day, hurrying back home to ensure that Max kept up his church attendance, well turned out of course. There was always a shadow lingering around them that could never be erased, but they had learned how to cope with it and plodded on in hope.

Tempus fugit, as they say, and with it time eased away on its cosmic journey. Max passed away, as did Fred's wife, Nora. Both were removed from the Presbyterian Church on the other side of the wall from Black's Lane to their place of rest. Max joined his son in the family plot, the second name labeling the headstone. Fred retired as a board member of his church, passing the baton to a younger successor. His and Francis's friendship continued unabated. They met for coffee, conversation, and a laugh, until Francis for health reasons relocated to be with daughter in England. They still kept in touch, exchange of cards at Christmas and other times and the occasional telephone call, although Francis was always mindful of running up Lily's bill.

A decade passed, and then so did Francis. Lily rang to tell Fred that she had died peacefully in her sleep. Putting the phone down reflecting on a wonderful friendship, Fred said a silent prayer of thanks, shed a tear, and asked a Catholic friend to light a candle in chapel for Francis.

Some months later, he took a phone call from Lily telling him the family had arranged a memorial service for Francis in her parish church and invited him to be their guest of honor. That was a very special day, for a very special woman, a day Fred would not have missed for anything.

The church was full—mostly of non-Catholics, that's how much Francis Ferguson was known and respected. The mass was celebrated in simple form with the celebrant taking as his theme for the homily "Love God, and your neighbor as yourself."

The priest spoke eloquently of Francis and the way she lived her faith, always being a good neighbor and friend; he said that faith wasn't just going to church every day or to confession every week. It wasn't a tick box of misdemeanors; faith's more than that; it has to be lived every day, just like Francis did. Concluding, he said, "If we love our neighbors as ourselves, we'll do a lot of good securing our own salvation at the same time. It's a no-brainer."

When the mass ended, Fred and Lily exchanged a lifetime's worth of loving embrace. Happy tears flowed. Fred was introduced to the extended family; the reminiscing and storytelling continued long into the evening.

It didn't end there, of course; Fred knew that Francis would still be keeping an eye on him wherever she was. The moments spent with Francis, he knew, would remain with him forever. They were life-changing moments like when war was declared or when peace was announced to a gasping world.

There was something about Francis that Fred didn't know. She didn't hide the fact that she was brought up as a reformed Presbyterian—a covenanter. It was just that it was her business, nobody else's. Her upbringing in a family of seven children in a rural community in the reformed Presbyterian tradition was strict. She didn't like it and couldn't understand why preachers had to shout so loud and so often to focus on the wrath of God. She had gradually tuned off, turned a deaf ear, and only went to church to keep up appearances. In her late teens working in the city, she went with a friend to church, as it turned out a Catholic church. It was a small church with atmosphere; she liked it. The homily preached that day was about loving God and your neighbor as yourself.

The rest, as far as Francis was concerned, was water under her bridge.

A Gentle Breeze Can Shake Barley

There are only ninety-two shopping days to Christmas, the huge public electronic information monitor on Main Street scrolled. It did as it was intended to do—caught my eye and gave me cause for pause. At that moment as my thoughts were with you, Margaret, I thought I might as well use my time to search for a Christmas card for you. I know what you're thinking—he's always ahead of the game. The truth is that I had time in hand; I was thinking of you back home in Donegal when the flashing monitor caught my eye and drew me in, otherwise who in his or her right mind would be thinking about Christmas in September, for goodness sake. Come on! Well, someone was, hence the message on the public information system!

Lots of customs have grown up around the Christmas festival such as: gift giving, the advent calendar, the advent wreath, caroling, church services, the special meal, Christmas rhymers, candle in the window, Christmas greeting cards, and the Christmas tree. The Christmas rhymers, here in Maryland USA known as mummers, are a rare sight nowadays and I think we're the poorer for it. I remember being Wee Johnny Funny, "the man who collects the money," and you were made up as Beelzebub when we went knocking on the neighbor's doors as Christmas rhymers, hoping to be invited in to perform, entertain, and perhaps be rewarded with an apple or an orange. Happy days! The customs that endure are the exchange of Christmas gifts and Christmas greetings. It was, I believe, the magi—the wonderfully wise men—who invented the art of Christmas gift giving. Drawn by a star to the birth of a babe in a manger, they brought wise gifts. But perhaps they knew more. As Auden in "For the Time Being: A Christmas Oratorio" put it:

> Child at whose birth we do obsequy
> For our tall errors of imagination,
> Redeem our talents with your little cry.

But who would have thought that the penny postal service introduced in 1840 coupled with the production of the first commercial Christmas card three years later would revolutionize the mode of exchanging Christmas greetings. Sadly it also heralded the advent of the commercialization of Christmas, slipped in under the radar like a thief in the night—a process that has continued with increasing intensity. Look at me, for goodness sake, browsing shops in search of Christmas cards in September. What more proof does anyone need?

Did you know, by the way, that Dickens' *A Christmas Carol* was published in 1843, the same year that the first commercial Christmas card was produced? Now there's food for thought.

Last Christmas all sorts of cards dropped through my letter box—charity thank-you cards, luxury cards, home-made cards, privately printed cards, institutional sponsorship cards, promotional cards, family photo cards e type cards, and cards not even remotely seasonal, that is if Christmastide is still classed as a season. I remember thinking then, *What's it all about? Have we lost the plot?*

Browsing, it dawned on me for the first time that the iconography on the commercial Christmas cards I was looking at hadn't changed much, if any since Victorian times. Not that I was around in Victorian times, but who knows, I might have morphed. The cards I was perusing, with increasing frustration, fell into four generic groups: aspects of the season represented by the red-breasted robin; Christmas activities, of which shopping topped the poll; Christmas traditions with Santa Claus supreme; and nativity scenes featuring a child in a manger. On one card the child was black! Was Jesus a black Jew? You know the thought had never occurred to me until just now. Isn't that incredible? Isaiah tells us that the virgin will conceive and bear a son, and he will be called Emmanuel, which means "God is with us!" But I have to tell you that what struck me forcefully was that the vast majority of Christmas cards on sale did not feature images related to the nativity. My little bit of ad hoc research suggested that there isn't much demand for or interest in the real story surrounding the birth of Jesus Christ.

Christmas in our multicultural, plural, diverse societies has become just another festival, a holiday period that has little or nothing to do with the birth of Jesus Christ. But the point is that Christmas is all about the birth of Jesus Christ, not the red-breasted robin, not shopping until we drop, or feasting. It has become, it seems, just a season of goodwill, bonhomie, good-hearted exchanges, back slapping, feasting and drinking, and preparation for the arrival of Santa Claus, and why not; there's nothing wrong with that; after all, "It's a time for children."

I don't know how you feel about it, but I think that we've been seduced by the relentless commercialization and materialism of Christmas, typified by invented events like the Black Friday syndrome. Not that I've ever queued overnight outside a store in pursuit of next morning's bargain. Our old weather-buffeted boats of inherited faith drift from shore to shore on commercially created currents of want and greed. Christmastide in the third millennium could well become a dead sea of materialism because of our collective Christian apathy.

My point is that Christmas is the Christian festival commemorating the birth of Jesus Christ—the timeless story of a couple's extraordinary personal journey in the development and spread of a radical idea. The birth of Jesus Christ was an event that split history forever. It divided time eternally in terms of before and after Christ. No other person in the history of this world can claim that distinction. The reality, the unvarnished truth, is that little if anything was idyllic about Jesus's coming into this world. If we would pause and think about the nativity story from a slightly different perspective, images that better correspond to reality might emerge.

Mary and Joseph, like many travelers, arrived at their destination, perhaps late at night, and sought a place to stay only to discover that all the hotels, inns, and boarding houses were full. Something big was on in town that weekend. We've all been there, haven't we? Maybe they were refused lodgings because someone didn't like the look of them; after all they weren't well dressed, had no baggage, were on foot, she a pregnant girl with an older man, riding on a donkey! Their social status would have been fairly obvious; they weren't wealthy, and decent accommodation was at a premium, way beyond their means. So they finished up sleeping rough. In our student days we often crashed in each other's places, remember? It was no big deal then, and it's no big deal now. Young people do it all the time. But a young pregnant girl riding on a donkey accompanied by an older man, that puts a different twist on it, don't you think?

Something that had been gently gnawing away at me for some time now, thanks to my Christmas card browsing for you, found release, like the genie from the proverbial lamp. It's simply that the nativity scenes depicted on Christmas cards on sale in the high street present the holy family as icons pre and post the birth of Jesus—unperturbed, beautiful, at peace, contented, happy, well dressed, angelic, and always at the ready to welcome visitors. There is no hint of poverty, fear, hardship, deprivation, or scandal; Mary and Joseph are presented cozy and content in a candlelit warm cave with farm animals for company. They don't capture or convey the reality of their situation. Commercial Christmas card art is a calculated, targeted, commercial appeal to feelings and emotions, especially maternal. Mary was greatly troubled and afraid because she was a virgin but was persuaded that she was the chosen one. At that moment of acknowledgment did she comprehend anything of the consequences that would flow from it? In her situation and her culture, is it possible at our distance in time, culture, and circumstance to even begin to contemplate how or what she felt? An unmarried pregnant teenager might! And who would believe her when she told them that she was with child by the Holy

Spirit! Her parents, Joseph her betrothed, her friends, her neighbors! Who would believe her today? If she lived next door to you or me, would we believe her? I have to say I don't think I would. Joseph, the original quiet man, apparently says nothing, never utters a sound, but being a person of integrity decided to divorce her informally, but later changed his mind. But what did Joseph say? How did he behave when Mary told him that she was made pregnant by the Holy Spirit? We have to guess, because none of what we really need to know is disclosed. Was he the least bit dubious? Think about it for just a moment. The small town of Nazareth was a labyrinth of lanes and alleyways, where news traveled faster than the speed of light; nothing was secret for long, and well-oiled tongues would wag as soon as Mary's condition became known. Remember our home village; news by jungle telegraph traveled fast there too. When Mary visited her cousin Elizabeth, both with child, there was rejoicing in Elizabeth's village at the miracle, but there is no mention in the Gospels of rejoicing in Nazareth. Joseph didn't have to take Mary with him to Bethlehem for the census, it was sufficient for him to be there as head of the household. But he took the heavily pregnant Mary on an arduous journey far away from home, family, and friends to be among strangers, in an unfamiliar village. Why? Was it to shield her from public humiliation?

Imagine the birthing scene in a stable surrounded by farm animals—the atmosphere, hygiene, sanitation, medical support, facilities primitive if any, hot water. Can we really more than two thousand years later even begin to imagine it? Impossible, unless of course we happened to be in similar circumstances in one of those awful refugee camps that stain humanity today.

We should remember that Mary and Joseph were on their own—no doctor, nurse, midwife—only the two of them. When the birthing process began, who delivered the baby Jesus? It had to be Joseph; no one else was there as far as we know. We don't know if it was an easy birth for a first time mother, but it must have been at the least a very scary experience for Mary and Joseph. Yet on Mary and Joseph's birthing experience of Jesus, scripture is silent. When the baby Jesus was safely delivered, Joseph

I presume cleaned Him up, wrapped Him in a blanket, readied Mary to receive Him, and presented Him into her arms. No doubt she felt the joy every mother feels when her child is born, and all is well. But what did she really feel in the marrow of her bones? Did she know then what the future held for her son? Did they weary through his growing up of the sorrow to come? There is so much we do not know about the family life of Mary, Joseph, and Jesus, as first Joseph and then Mary are airbrushed out of the story. What age was Jesus when his earthly father died? What did Jesus feel when Joseph his earthly father died? What did he do? What did he say? Did he grieve? We don't know because the storytellers don't tell us. What walks did father and son take together? What did, could, Joseph, a simple craftsman, teach his son Jesus?

The question for me is simply what do we learn from reading Luke's gospel about the birth of Jesus Christ? The manger; the Christmas crib, an animal feeding trough elevated above all others in history. Churches make elaborate cribs; I've seen them constructed as hierarchical, linear structures, and cozy stable tableaus, beautifully lit and enhanced with atmospheric music, before which people are often encouraged to pray. They all have animals too, all sorts of animals, but where is the evidence that animals were present at the birth of Jesus? The whole point of the manger in the story is that it was given to the shepherds as a sign; it indicated where the baby they were searching for would be found.

There is much about Christmas as presented and invented that blinds us to the truth. We were fortunate enough to be nourished by many good teachers when growing up, but Mary, Joseph, and family have much to teach humanity; unfortunately the fullness of their journey together was not recorded, and our world is the poorer for it. Perhaps it was thought that to record their family life experiences would divert attention from what was actually happening—divine intervention in the trajectory of world affairs through the birth of Jesus Christ. I wonder how much more enriched we would be, had scriptures told us more about their family life, especially in these times when marriage and family are under constant assault.

The real challenge of Christmas surely is simply to believe and in believing not to rinse out the reality of a pregnant teenager and her lover in difficult times. Commercial Christmas card iconography and church cribs do not inform, enlighten, or challenge my belief about the nativity. But then no single image on any Christmas card or church crib could possibly capture the complete journey in faith of Mary and Joseph. But there is something often overlooked in this story. Simeon was the first person other than Mary and Joseph to grasp the significance of what God had set in motion. I don't know what, if any, their connection with Simeon was, other than that they met by chance in the temple, but his reaction on encountering the infant Jesus was one of liberation.

So the bottom line is I didn't choose a Christmas card for you. In fact I left the Main Street so disappointed and disgruntled that I've decided not to send any Christmas cards to anyone ever again. Ironically it's not just the mind-numbing images; it's becoming too costly to send them. Now there's a twist in the tale—the mode of exchanging Christmas greetings changed forever by the introduction of the penny postal service in 1840 is now slowly but surely, because of the increasing cost of postage, being replaced as the mode of choice by email.

So my Christmas greeting this year from me to you, Margaret, is in the form of a word picture contained in Auden's "Christmas Oratorio."

At the manger Mary speaks:

> What have you learned from the womb that bore you
> But an anxiety your father cannot feel?
> Sleep. What will the flesh that I gave do for you,
> Or my mother love, but tempt you from His will?
> Why was I chosen to teach His Son to weep?
> In your first few hours of life here, O have you
> Chosen already what death must be your own?
> How soon will you start on your Sorrowful Way?

Remember? Of course you don't; wouldn't expect you to, Margaret. So there you have it; my Christmas greeting to you this year is contained in your Christmas gift to me way back in 1994—a book of Auden's collected poems. You'll have to do a bit of work yourself to find the word picture I am sending you, but I've given you a clue where to start looking. Enjoy the search. I think you'll find it's worth the effort. I suppose that's the moral; Christians need to reclaim Christmas and in so doing search for meaning and inspiration. Let's see if your word picture in Auden's "Christmas Oratorio" work matches mine.

It all happened a long time ago, beyond the compass of memory. Things change; understanding evolves; boundaries shift.

When I left home a generation ago, Ireland was perceived as a priest-ridden society; conservative steadfast, rigid, inward looking, sure of itself, confident of its faith trajectory. Yet in an incredibly short time, a generation, it has become a diverse, multicultural, outward-looking, liberal society and an integral part of the European experiment. Did anyone see it coming as we entered the third millennium?

In May 2018 the Irish people removed the Eighth Amendment to the Constitution that provided for equal rights to the mother and the unborn child, resetting the Constitution as it was two decades ago. Then in October 2018 they also voted to remove blasphemy as an offense from their Constitution. From what I hear, there is more to come on women's rights within the home too. And why not?

Northern Ireland, by way of contrast, is the only part of the United Kingdom where abortion is illegal in almost every conceivable circumstance with the Presbyterians standing resolute. It seems to me that the Presbyterians are now the latter-day Catholics! Now there's a thought. But a gentle breeze can shake the barley there too.

Mary and Joseph lived over two millennia ago in a society with political, cultural, economic, and religious boundaries that from a far distance it is impossible for us to even begin to contemplate. Our environment shapes us.

Will Ireland be a poorer place in years to come? I hope not.

As Auden put it:

> If I could tell you I would let you know.

An Odd Fate

It was a midsummer morning when he set about the garden chores planned the night before. The sun had moved almost overhead when he finished. Noon was nigh. The lawns front and back were cut, edges trimmed, borders tidied, potted plants watered, and in the small greenhouse the tomato, chili, and other plants had also been given due attention. It was time for a welcome cup of tea and a rest.

The shrubs he had planted many years ago had now matured. His favorite was the *Cotoneaster cornubria*. It was very small, insignificant when he planted it; now it was over seven meters high with a huge canopy providing welcome, cool, dappled shade from the noonday sun. He headed for the seat he had built under its overhanging branches forming an arbor of tranquility and privacy; it was his sanctum—his favorite place in the garden.

The birds and the bees loved the cotoneaster too. It had budded early; the canopy was a mass of small white and rose-tinted flowers, alive with buzzing bees collecting their bounty of nectar. As the summer eased into autumn, the rich green variegated leaves turned deep scarlet, and the abundant flowers would metamorphose into red berries. When autumn bowed to greet winter, the red berries ripened and turned yellow, and the birds feasted.

As he sat down book in hand, deposited there earlier in anticipation of this special moment, his wife, Peggy, appeared on cue tray in hand with tea for two. It was a well-rehearsed dance, this get-together in the garden at noon for tea. In the surround sound of birdsong, they sat quietly enjoying their togetherness. The air vibrated with bird music as the tits, sparrows, finches, and robins flitted between the birdseed holders sited around the garden. It reminded him of the pick and mix stalls in food halls. The birds had a routine; they would visit the birdseed holders and the canopy of berries in a particular sequence at certain times of the day in season. Some of them were finicky.

Apart from the constant bird twittering, all was quiet and peaceful until it was time for Peggy to abandon him to his book, in favor of her meditation class. When she had gone, he settled back, picked up his book, and thumbed it open.

The poem he had happened on was Larkin's "This Be the Verse":

> They fuck you up, your mum and dad.
> They may not mean to, but they do.
> They fill you with the faults they had
> And some extra, just for you.
>
> Man hands on misery to man.
> It deepens like a coastal shelf.
> Get out as early as you can,
> And don't have any kids yourself.

Paul skimmed through the short poem; it was bland to his taste, like the sensitivity of a sulky teenager. He put a finger to his tongue for wetness, to leaf the page, and tasted dried mud in the process, as his eyes riveted unto the last line of the poem, "And don't have any kids yourself."

The word *kids* in the last line caught his attention; he abhorred it used as surrogate for children. *Maybe I'm just a traditionalist after all*, he thought. Paul and Peggy, with five children of their own and seven grandchildren, had unwittingly ignored Larkin's exhortation, and he was extremely glad they had. He believed that parents didn't meaningfully, purposely damage their children; nobody could be that cruel surely. But he also knew that parents could not help but leave their indelible imprint on the shaping of their children. His received wisdom was that it mostly came from a good place, a deeply embedded instinct to see them survive and thrive. He rinsed his mind to read the poem again, this time methodically, critically in pursuit of depth of meaning and enlightenment. As he read it a second time, his mother's mantra leaped into his mind, tore at his heart, and stole away his peace: "Your parents ruin the first half of your life, and your children ruin the rest." How many times at his mother's side had he heard that? He was glad Peggy was not beside him just now, although now was when he needed her most. He was trembling inside, feeling shredded, in tatters, but with gritted teeth he read it again, a third time, exploring every word, savoring every nuance, feeling conflicted and increasingly emotional.

He closed the book and set it aside, pulled himself together, straightened his back, sat upright on the seat, and started the breathing exercises he used to relax when emotionally stressed. With every breath he exhaled he felt the ocean of emotion inside subside until it became the tranquil sea that enabled him to think calmly.

Paul was the youngest of thirteen children. Like steps of stairs, the neighbors would often say. As he grew older he never could figure out in the stair analogy what step was his, the top or the bottom—a conundrum he revisited every time he encountered stairs. It didn't matter much really; he was just a child trying to make sense of things people said, like, "I'll warm your ears for you," meaning administering a cuff on the ear.

His father was a bus driver; his mother was a seamstress. Hard-working parents though they were, it was a struggle at times to make ends meet. In their home, today's must-have necessities—television, washing machine, dishwasher, microwave oven—were luxuries. Not many working-class homes had cars at their doors then either. Thankfully times had changed.

As the baby of the family, he was always by his mother's apron, especially in the mornings when work and school beckoned the others, and their terraced house emptied to peace and quiet. That was when he saw his mother, bent over the jar box known today in polite society as a

Belfast sink, cold water running from the single tap, scrubbing the heaps of discarded clothing on the washing board, big blocks of Sunlight soap at the ready. He remembered the cold winter's mornings he helped her carry the heavy basins of washing out into the small enclosed yard to the mangle, stood on a wooden box and turned the wheel with its big wooden handle, as she fed the washing through the rollers and watched fascinated as the squeezed-out water trickled cheerfully down into the yard drain. *Children know how to stay in the moment*, he thought. *No need to teach them mindfulness; they just live it.* Once the dye in a garment had run, the mangle-liberated water oozed out red, like blood; it frightened him. His mother laughed his fear away. On wet days she would hang the clothes inside on an overhead wooden rack raised and lowered by cords strung through pulleys. Decades later, much to his amusement, the humble scrubbing board was elevated to percussion musical instrument status with the arrival of the cult of skiffle.

He couldn't recall when he first heard her mantra: "Your parents ruin the first half of your life, and your children ruin the rest," but he was sure he heard it when she was doing the never-ending washing, baking griddles of bread, or peeling mountains of potatoes—tasks she did unseen every day, him by her side always. He took it all in, absorbed it, recorded it in his memory banks, and stored it safely away, but he didn't know then that he was doing it. She had said it so many times to him that a sense of blame penetrated and lodged so deeply in his inner self that he felt responsible for her sadness and discontent. That reveal surfaced much later.

As they grew older together, her shoulders rounded, her back hunched, and her breathing coarsened and labored. He was an ever present witness, as her face aged and hair whitened unnoticed by the others. He felt her pain, her disappointments, and often wondered were all her music had gone—the hopes and dreams that must have filled her young bride's heart. He knew she had never envisaged or contemplated the life of continuous drudgery that was her life then, as he saw it.

One morning sitting on the clapped-out sofa in their back room, tired and weary, she confided to herself, "I never knew it would be like this; I never wanted thirteen children," and quietly sobbed. She had forgotten, tired and wearied, that he was there until he reached up and took her hand and innocently said, "Don't cry, Mammy. I'm here; it'll be all right." His reward was a big hug. Then together they got on with the rest of their day; not another word was said about it, but that moment seared him forever; it never left him.

It was not all drudgery, he knew that. His parents occasionally would go to the "pictures," as it was called then, and when they could, they went on family day trips to the seaside, but holidays away were nonessentials, not affordable, something to dream about. So as a family unit, the societal glue, they plodded on constrained by a handed-down religious belief system. Call it faith if you will. But like all faiths simple and dogmatic to an outsider perhaps, but soothing, comforting sustaining maybe to the insider. A simpler faith it could not have been. Fettered and shackled by doctrine and dogma rooted in a theology that beyond a penny catechism instruction had never been explained to them, not that they would have understood Christian theology articulated in the language of theologians. It was a simple faith that denied them the freedom to shape their own lives, so they carried on silently, dutifully, docilely bearing the crosses in life that came their way, in the unfailing hope that somehow it merited their eternal salvation.

As Paul's character and emotional shaping progressed, he became more and more sensitized to his siblings; he was softer and gentler than them. They thought him too day dreamy—not with it, not in the real world, a bit of a mammy's boy. That hurt him deeply; he didn't show it, kept it inside, hidden. As he grew older, he began to understand the family culture that had gradually developed and stealthily enveloped them all. His siblings communicated obliquely, never shared their feelings or confidences. It was an Alice in Wonderland environment where no meant yes, and yes meant no, and he was the mad hare. To converse you had to know the code, the rules. Paul's problem was that he never fully understood the cultural rules; he felt like a sunflower searching for its sun, a mushroom in a derelict shed straining toward a keyhole of light.

He was very young when his father passed away and didn't remember much about it other than a lot of people called at the house. His father was a good provider, kept a roof over their heads and food on the table. He worked weekends and summer holidays to earn "extra dough," he would say. *That in a few words*, thought Paul, *was all he could say about his father*; *pathetic really*.

As the baby of the family, Paul had spent the most emotionally charged moments of his entire life at his mother's apron, but he wasn't tied to it. He witnessed her emotional turmoil, aging and wearying. It pained him greatly, but as he grew older he understood that there was an enormous chasm between recognizing and sharing his mother's anguish, and suffering it. Those trained to deal with the pain of others knew the cutoff point; otherwise they would be overwhelmed and incapable of functioning appropriately. That moment of realization was his liberation. He had without training or help of any kind found his cutoff point. He would share, but he would not bear his mother's pain.

Over time his siblings left home and went their different ways, firmly molded. It was a mold too constraining for Paul; he was determined to smash it into smithereens and break free. Paul lived with his mother; they had the family home all to themselves. It was a different place now quiet, tension free. "Still at the apron Paul" his siblings would jibe whenever they occasionally called in, oblivious of the hurt delivered. It wasn't deliberate, he knew that; they didn't know they were doing it, but it didn't sooth his feelings. He had read somewhere that there were two kinds of children: those born to repay their parents and those born to take from their parents. He thought about his siblings and into which category they would fall when his mother's passing came to be, but he put that thought away; it was too destructive. Anyway there was nothing to take; she had given freely all of herself to all of them anyway in equal shares. When her passing came, he would deal with it as he had always dealt with the things none of his siblings would deal with—her wishes would prevail; he would see to that. In the passing years he was seldom invited to his siblings' homes, family celebrations, or anything remotely family. Although he knew they loved each other deeply, showing it was something they just didn't do.

One day by chance he met one of his nieces down the town. She seemed uptight, tense, and bothered about something, but as they small-talked over coffee her face softened; she relaxed and started talking freely and openly. They sat together drinking coffee well into late afternoon bolstered by three top-ups without even realizing it. As they parted he knew that all she wanted was someone she could talk to, someone to trust, someone to listen. His siblings had taken their family culture with them and infected their children with it. He had worked diligently at listening because he had not been listened to, not heard, not understood in his own home. After meeting with his niece, he resolved that if he was ever blessed with children he would converse with them openly, honestly, and directly; there would be no Alice in Wonderland stuff. *But old habits die hard,* he thought. *They need to be worked on every day.*

When his mother's growing weariness became serious illness, it was clear that her time to pass over was not far away. She was ready in herself; church readied too, with the last rites administered, the attending priest told Paul there's nothing more anyone can do but pray with her.

Custom and practice compelled her family to sit with her until she took her leave of them. They all gathered and stood around her bed shuffling their feet in a slow dance of embarrassment or sat enduring their awkwardness as best they could, until it became so unbearable that one by one they sought fresh air or relief and left her bedroom. There was no outward display of feelings, just the occasional meaningless sterile utterances. Signs of grief, sadness, and sorrow would find expression in public at her funeral. The public perception of family unity and cohesion would be preserved.

Paul sat beside his mother, her hand in his. He didn't mind if it made them feel uneasy; they would get over it. His feelings were out there, and he was glad. Death comes slowly sometimes to the very frail. The body refuses to give up even after the will to live has let go. So it was with his mother.

It was late on the fourth night's sitting that his mother passed. There was only Paul and two of his siblings sitting in the room with her; they were asleep. His mother's breathing had become noticeably more labored—big, long, slow intakes of air, followed by long pauses and then very long slow exhalations. He knew she would pass when her heart gave up. He turned away from his mother to dampen a cloth to cool her face; when he turned back to her, she was gone. He had only taken his eyes off her for a second, but she was gone. There was nothing he could do; he was helpless, speechless, not that there was anything he could have done or said. His mother hadn't opened her eyes for three days and nights. He knew she wanted away, out of "this vale tears" as the prayer she often recited described life. A sense of loss swept over and engulfed him. He found himself in an emotional whirlpool; he sought blackness first—the inky blackness of the deepest coal mine he could find. How long he wrestled with his knotted emotions and feelings he didn't know. It was when someone behind him asked, "How is she?" and he in a state of bewilderment answered, "She's gone," did he come back to the reality of the moment and face it. The emptiness! The sleepers wanted to know why they weren't wakened. "Sorry, there just wasn't time; she didn't wait. She just went," he said, and then hands on head he wept.

Paul made all the funeral arrangements and executed her wishes as she had asked him to do; her meager estate was shared among her children. The family home was left to Paul, and when all the dust was settled, he set about getting on with the rest of his life. He had not yet turned twenty-one years of age, but he felt older, beaten and bullied by life, reared in a big family, hung over with a weight of loneliness that was almost unbearable. He knew he had to make the effort to climb out of his cesspit of hopelessness and leave all the pain and hurt behind if he was to reshape and make something of his life.

After the funeral service, interment beside his father completed, and the gathering for shared refreshments had wearied itself to a dreary conclusion, Paul found himself exhausted and alone back in the family home—his home without really knowing how he had got there. It was as if he was on automatic pilot. The reality of the moment disturbed him. The house was deadly silent, empty, and smaller without her presence. Wandering from room to room opening cupboards and drawers, he rummaged around in vain for some tangible sensation of her, but he could find it not; only memories remained. As the house seemed to get smaller around him, he realized that what was once the heart of it had gone, never to return. He went out into the enclosed yard and stood in the darkness of the night feeling utterly alone and completely empty. It started to rain; there was no wind, just soft rain easing gently down on his head and caressing his face, bringing peace. That's when he felt her spirit close.

In the kitchen, a cup of tea in hand, he thought about his future. It was time for him to reach out, discover, and let his true self see the light of day. He was free to go and free to do; his life was not on hold anymore. He knew that a different approach to life was needed—more philosophical perhaps; cautiously going forward, there would be much to learn and relearn in building new relationships. In his heart he was up for it.

Work colleagues introduced him to golf, which he took up with enthusiasm, joined the local club, and within eighteen months his handicap was in single figures. Then an opening presented for him to join a Saturday morning four-ball. Paul loved it—enjoyed the company and the good-natured bantering—and looked forward to it every week. Most of all he loved playing in the club competitions. Golf was not a team game; it was one player against another over the same course—each player making his or her own decisions, playing his or her own ball each and every shot. He was fiercely competitive. Golf challenged his reserved nature and levered him out of himself in an extraordinary way. As a person he blossomed.

There was another aspect of golf that attracted him. In the summer months, Paul would be waiting when the greenkeepers opened up the course at five o'clock in the morning. He would play and practice on his own; he loved the early mornings. The sun would be rising; the summer visiting swallows would be on the wing feeding; buzzards would be hovering over the woods hunting for breakfast; and up on the heather-covered hills the ascending larks would be singing, just for him he liked to think, but he knew better. Over time he got to recognize the individual pheasants as they strutted around marking out their territories with their raucous calls to each other in the process. Once he saw a peregrine falcon take a pigeon right in front of him on the ninth fairway. How he regretted he didn't have his camera with him that day. He loved the vast emptiness of the course in the early morning, the sheer scale of it, and the freedom. At times he felt as if he owned it. In every way it was his cathedral. Often on the golf course on early summer mornings he hovered in his mind somewhere between the mystery of earth and sky, and the longer he hovered, the vastness between them somehow grew smaller.

He was on one of his solo early-morning golfing forays standing on the seventeenth tee on the back nine, level par for his round, at about eight thirty in the morning. It was a beautiful summer's morning—the sun was up, not a cloud in the bright blue sky, barely a breeze, and nature, it seemed, was at peace with itself. The seventeenth hole was a par five dogleg left, trees on the right, no trouble down the left. As he teed up he had a weird feeling of a presence, like someone was watching him. He backed off his drive, had a look around, saw no one, and addressed his ball again, but still the feeling persisted. It felt odd, bizarre. Unsettled, his concentration disturbed, he drove his tee shot into the trees on the right. In anger and frustration he thumped his club into the ground. He took another ball from his bag, teed up again, and without thinking hammered the ball miles straight down the fairway. Feeling a lot better, he shoved his club into his bag, shouldered it, and strode angrily off the tee.

Approaching the trees on the right his anger subsided; he climbed over the barbed wire fence to look, iron in hand, among the trees for his first ball. Searching a few meters just inside the tree line proved fruitless. About twenty meters further in, he was confronted in a clearing by a big white dog staring straight at him, slowly but steadily wagging its tail to and fro, its big slobbering tongue dangling from the side of its mouth. He could see its teeth, and underneath, between its big front paws, his ball. Instinctively, defensively, he took a tighter grip on his seven iron. Dog and man stood and confronted each other. After what seemed a long time, the deadlock was broken when a voice called out, "Orian, come here, you big dope." The dog acknowledged the voice with a slight move of its enormous head and then reluctantly ambled off toward it. He was still stationary when the same voice said, "I'm sorry about that; he wouldn't hurt a fly, the big softie." Paul looked to his left and saw a little way down below him a young woman about his age standing on the tarmac path that bordered the public country park.

In that moment of first sight he was drawn into her presence; strangely she didn't seem at all out of place. She had dark wavy hair tumbling down to her shoulders, bushy eyebrows, piercing blue eyes, and a smiling face. From head to toe she wore blue—, runners, jeans and fleece. She had an aura about her that fascinated him and drew him in.

The spell was broken when she said, "Enjoy your golf," waved and turned and walked away. Paul stood and watched her as she went on her way; the tumbling wave of her dark hair, the roll of her shoulders, the swing of her hips and her bouncy walk—harmony in motion until she was out of sight. When she had gone, he slowly exhaled, gathered himself together, retrieved his ball, and headed back out onto the golf course.

He was still thinking about his encounter in the trees as he approached his second ball on the seventeenth fairway. He had never driven a ball this far down before. Mind now back in golfing mode, he figured maybe he could make the green in two. If he did, it would the first time he did that at this par five. His two wood in hand, he lined up his shot and smashed the ball straight as an arrow onto the seventeenth green to within two meters of the pin. Paul was jubilant, on in two; close to the pin, a first eagle beckoning, he couldn't believe it. He took his time over the putt; the greens hadn't been cut yet, and there was still moisture on the grass; the putt would move left to right, he knew, but how much? That was the question. All the mental calculations done, he lined up the putt, struck the ball, and watched it roll and roll toward the hole and die into the cup. He stood on the green and loudly cheered himself. What a play, tee to green, forgetting that it was his second ball and forgetting his encounter in the trees. But it was nonetheless a great par save. He figured it was just meant to be his day, today; some days were like that—fated. Except it wasn't quite like that, at least not as he expected; he left the eighteenth green with a double bogey on his card, two over for his round.

Driving home he mulled over the strange sequence of events from tee to green on the seventeenth hole. The eerie feeling someone was watching him; hitting the ball into the trees, something he had never done before; coming face-to-face with a huge white dog and meeting the young woman; and to cap it all making his first eagle on the seventeenth green. *Am I dreaming?* he wondered. *Will I wake up wondering what it was all about?* Since his mother's passing he had recurring dreams in which he was always frantically looking for his house or car keys until he woke up and found them where he had put them on the bedside cabinet. He had never figured out what they meant, if anything, but they had gradually faded away. He was home before he knew it, wondering as he had done after his mother's funeral how on earth he had got there. It was weird. More was to follow. As he reached to unlock his front door, he found himself staring at the brass numerals on the door displaying number seventeen. Closing the door quietly behind him, he could not help feeling that the sequence of events on the seventeenth hole was somehow preordained. It was an odd feeling that lingered.

Several weeks later on a Saturday afternoon, Paul was in the local library browsing through the travel section, searching for something on Venice; it was on his must go to visit list. The fairytale network of canals, the architecture, the narrow bridges linking expansive squares, the majestic churches, the art within them, and the amazing frescos on building facades all appealed to his romantic nature. Absorbed in his task, he had made a gap on the bookshelf. In the throes of replacing the removed books he found himself looking straight at the young woman he had encountered in the woods a few weeks ago. He was taken aback and showed it. She just smiled and said, "Fancy meeting you here. How are you?"

From somewhere Paul found a voice. "Fine, nice to see you again too," he replied.

"Going somewhere nice?" she asked.

"I was looking for something on Venice. I've always wanted to go there, but there's nothing here," Paul said.

"Sorry," she said, holding up two travel books. "I've got them. I was just about to take them out."

"Oh," Paul muttered, a shadow of disappointment masking his face. Still smiling she said, "Why don't we sit in here somewhere and browse through them together. You might find one that appeals to you more than the other and me likewise; then we'll both be happy."

Finding a quiet spot in the library wasn't difficult. Time quickly slipped away, so quickly in fact that they were still engaged in reading and chatting as the library closing time loomed. Looking at his watch, feeling more at ease with himself, Paul suggested they could go for coffee and finish what they were doing. It was seven o'clock in the evening when Peggy left Paul to visit her parents but only after they had arranged to meet again.

They continued meeting, getting to know each other, and slowly revealing bit by bit their inner selves. They were so unalike in many ways. Peggy was an only child living at home with her parents; she had grown up lonely for siblings. Paul had lots of siblings, but he too had experienced loneliness. She was outgoing, full of life, and exuberant, while he was reserved, shy. He was trying to reshape his life; she was enjoying hers.

Eighteen months after their first odd encounter, they were married. Paul sold the family home; he and Peggy bought a place of their own and set up home, a home they never ever had any desire to leave. From the outset they had talked about having children; Peggy wanted many, but Paul was more cautious. In the end they had five children: three boys and two girls.

Paul's own upbringing had made him concerned about his fatherliness; he had striven to reshape his life, and he desperately wanted to be a positive influence in the shaping of his children's lives. Peggy could and would, but could he? It niggled at him; he knew the more he would try to shape his children's lives the more difficult and strained their relationship might become. He would have to rely a lot on Peggy's innate common sense. To be a good father, he would adopt the persona of a gardener. Prepare the ground—he had worked at that—sow the seed, watch it sprout, nurture the plant, let it grow at its own pace, and don't force it. When it needed a little support now and then, provide it; shelter it from the frost of life when required; in time it would develop a sturdy stem and provide rich produce. He had learned on the job, as it were, and with seven grandchildren he was still learning.

Sitting now under the cotoneaster thinking back over past decades, he laughed out loud and thought how utterly ludicrous. Today was their eldest grandchild's fifteenth birthday, and Peggy, as always, had arranged the traditional celebration garden party. That was the real reason he was tidying up the garden before the clan gathered. It was the clatter of feet, the chattering voices, and the banging of the garden gate that alerted him. They were here already, and he wasn't ready. He was supposed to have set up the barbecue and tables; he would be in the doghouse now.

They had a dog, a big white one; by any stretch of the imagination, it was for Paul an odd fate. But he was very happy. It was then he recalled a poem, a parody of Larkin's by Adrian Mitchell:

> They tuck you up, your mum and dad
> They give you Peter Rabbit too.
> They give you all the treats they had
> And add some extra just for you.

He couldn't remember it all but, yes the last verse;

> Man hands on happiness to man
> It deepens like a coastal shelf,
> So love your parents all you can
> And have some cheerful kids yourself

Yes, *much better than Larkin's*, he thought as he went arms outstretched to welcome his family.

Another Perspective

It was one of those cold wet April mornings. Jack's wife, Mary, had gone shopping leaving him comfortably installed on his reclining armchair nestled in the bay widow recess of their cottage. He watched her back disappearing down the herring-boned paved garden path that stretched to their front gate and the world beyond. Jack always sat there when he had something to think about—to ponder.

Outside the fading light of the morning cast long shadows over the herbaceous-bordered pathway and manicured front lawn that was his pride and joy. The sky was busy forming black ominous clouds. Then the rain came; big heavy dollops of water plummeted from the skies pounding the grateful dry earth. Jack watched fascinated as the garden path soaked up the rainwater until it could absorb no more, and the thread of a stream began to form. Bits of garden debris on the path were soon overwhelmed and borne away by a mini tsunami, as it gathered momentum and surged joyfully down the brick paved path. The scene was mesmerizing, a metaphor for life, *Go with the flow.* He smiled at the thought and wished he had at times. But, *tempus fugit*, time passes; no point in looking back. Always look forward was Jack's mantra.

Jack was still wrapped in thought when Mary appeared at the mouth of the garden path laden with shopping. She was holding a heavy-looking bag in her left hand, while clamping something with her left arm against her side. In her right hand she grappled with a half opened umbrella and a bunch of keys. All the way down the garden path she was bullied by wind and relentless rain. Jack roused from his reverie and went to help, but just as he opened the front door, he heard a loud thud. His heart leaped into his mouth. He thought Mary had slipped and fallen. When he flung the door open, she was standing bedraggled, her feet drowning in a puddle of yellow egg yolk mess. She looked pathetic.

The something clamped under her left arm was a carton of organic eggs that she dropped when stretching, bunch of keys in hand to open the front door. What a sight; what a mess, but what a relief; she had not fallen. She was in one piece. Wisely Jack suppressed the temptation to laugh. He said nothing. *Best to hold my tongue*, he thought, and reaching out took the heavy bag of shopping from her, glad that it was only a dozen eggs that were smashed.

In the kitchen he put the kettle on and made tea while Mary regained her composure, changed into dry clothes, and slippered her feet. Sipping her tea, Mary laughed at her own foolishness as she explained to Jack that she was trying to open the door herself because she didn't want to disturb him. Jack laughed too; anxiety and tension quietly drifted away. The rain continued to pelt down outside, as they sat confident in the togetherness and warmth of shared silence.

As Jack mulled over what had just happened, he wondered what influence he had, if any, that would cause Mary to balk from disturbing him. He wasn't working at anything; he wasn't reading. He was enjoying watching the morning tsunami growing in his garden. It occurred to him that people do this kind of thing all the time with groceries and baggage of all kinds. They could not, would not, either set their baggage aside or ask for help. They clung on tightly to it even though they hurt themselves one way and another in the process. Focusing on what Mary had said about not wanting to disturb him, he wondered if it was possible to care too much. No, it wasn't that; he told himself; she was very considerate, not smothering; she had an independent streak in her, but sometimes she thought too much about the other person. For a long time "think of the other person" had been her mantra, which he endorsed with a caveat of prudence. Satisfied that it was innate, not something he was demanding or forcing, the thought that perhaps he should be thinking of the other person too a little more flitted momentarily across his mind.

With the tea finished and the table cleared, they set about the process of cleaning up the mess outside "before," Mary said, "anyone comes to the door." Not that they were overwhelmed with callers since the last of their three children had gotten married and left home. They lived quietly below the radar getting on with their lives. They had a diverse active social life but when at home they left the world outside while they read and listened to music they liked. The rain induced mini tsunami, had helped a lot. The eggs, if not free range before, now were free flowing, and that reminded him of their cruise up the Yellow River some years ago. Another notion Jack thought best to keep to himself. When the cleanup was completed to Mary's satisfaction, she set about unpacking the shopping and preparing lunch. Jack knew it was time to disappear because Mary liked the kitchen to herself; he was too messy.

Back in his favorite spot and settled in his comfortable armchair, Mary's incident at the door focused Jack's thoughts on thresholds—the everyday thresholds people navigate through life. When he heard the thud outside the door, he was sure Mary had fallen and that she would have hurt herself. He couldn't bear the thought of it. What relief he felt when she was standing there in front of him instead of lying sprawled in a heap on the doorstep.

That's when his thoughts turned to another incident on another day. It was the day they went on an outing with their three children—Phillip, Florence, and Joseph—to a forest park they had never visited before. Phillip had his eighth birthday the day before; Florence was younger by two years, and Joseph had just turned four. It was a lovely day full of promise when they set off, but most of all he wanted the children to see the red squirrels cavorting through forest canopy at lightning speed and maybe feeding at the feeding stations provided up in the trees by the forest rangers.

Phillip, a boisterous little boy, dashed about among the trees disturbing any wildlife that might have been there and in the process significantly reducing the chances of spotting any red squirrels. He would run off down the trail in front of them, hide behind a tree until they approached, and then jump out to frighten Florence if he could. He played this game over and over again, with all the mischievous energy he could muster. As they walked along still hoping for a sighting of the red squirrels the trail climbed upward, gently at first, but as they meandered along, the gradient increased. Approaching the top of the incline Phillip, as usual galloped off ahead of them and disappeared, leaving them thinking, *He's at it again; he'll be hiding somewhere waiting to pounce when we least expect it.*

When they crested the hill a little later and looked down, they saw to their horror Phillip standing in the middle of a rickety old wooden bridge that spanned a river flowing fast beneath it. The decking of the bridge was made with four-inch-wide boards irregularly spaced along its length. There were wide gaps in the decking; some boards were missing. The bridge, if that is what it could be called, didn't have handrails or side barriers or anything. It was simply a crude decking across the river about thirty feet long. It was dangerous. Phillip was standing in the middle of it, gleefully shouting up at them, "look at me; look at me," waving his arms excitedly as the river rushed beneath him.

Before Mary could utter a sound, Jack muttered between clenched teeth, "Don't utter a sound; stand still. Keep his attention on you while I walk down and get to him; we don't want to start him running off again." Mary stood rock still clinging onto Florence and Joseph with a grip of fear in each hand.

Phillip was waving excitedly up to his mother as Jack inched slowly along the rickety bridge, calmly talking to Phillip, distracting him all the while, until he reached him and gathered him into his arms, thanking God for his safe deliverance. Jack carried Phillip back to join his mother and siblings, vowing never to let him out of his sight again. Relieved, tragedy averted, they slowly retraced their steps back to their car and headed home. In the days that followed they talked over the incident. They blamed themselves—their naiveté and parental inexperience—and questioned their competence, capability, and fitness for parenthood. Their soul-searching continued unabated for weeks and months with increased acuity for their children's well-being. An outing on a day full of promise could easily have ended in disaster on a bridge in a country forest park. It was a threshold moment that they would never forget. They didn't see any red squirrels on their way back to their car, but then they had other things to think about.

That was a long time ago, Jack thought. He had come to realize he couldn't wrap his children up in cotton wool. They didn't recognize thresholds; they just took them in their stride and continued journeying through life. Why should they? After all, in the seven ages of man, they are characteristically free of baggage. Baggage gathering is all before them.

As Jack pondered these thoughts, he realized that the thresholds encountered in life come in many shapes and forms—physical, psychological, emotional, social, and economic. They can be a means of easy access or barriers to be overcome; steps and stairs confronting the mobility impaired; spiral stairs spinning people's thoughts in a whirlpool of emotion. As his thoughts surged and fermented, he compiled in his mind a list of potential thresholds (e.g., thresholds of pain, joy, sorrow, boredom, class, poverty, regret, failure, hurt, life, the list was never ending). No baby exiting the womb could possibly know it was crossing the threshold of life. Neither could the baby know that the door of the threshold of life swung both ways to facilitate access and egress.

Then it dawned on Jack that the pressing threshold he needed to address and conquer was simplicity; he needed to see things as they really are. As his thoughts rambled around the notion of thresholds, he began to think of them as exterior and interior, environmentally embedded and person centered. Every person, he reasoned, has a set of inner places that is inaccessible to others harboring thresholds that sooner or later may have to be confronted. This was the moment when from deep within himself Jack knew that it took a great deal of courage, determination, and persistence to cross some thresholds. *Therein lies the challenge, for me,* Jack thought. *You just don't think your way through thresholds. It's not a thinking task; it's a doing task. Thresholds are there to be crossed.* The thought imploded in his mind. It was his Damascus moment.

So engrossed in his thoughts was Jack that he hadn't noticed that the storm had abated, on its way to finding peace and tranquility. The rain had stopped; the surface of the garden path was bone dry, and the sun had moved southward on its journey across the now brightening sky. The pattern of shadows across the front garden and pathway had also changed, informing him from observation and experience that lunch was in the offing. Lunch was a simple egg-free affair, over which Mary regaled him with bits and pieces of her morning's shopping experiences—who she met, including those only too glad to unload their baggage on anyone willing to lend an ear. Jack had frequently advised that when she saw the usual suspects appearing, she should cross to the other side of the street but had given up on that job as Mary continued to pursue what she called her ministry of listening.

Now at ease with herself, second cup of tea in hand, Mary asked, "I suppose you are looking forward to your big day tomorrow?"

"Sure," Jack replied, "like looking forward to going to the dentist except that I've been to the dentist quite a few times and know what to expect; tomorrow is just a little bit different."

"Ah, sure," Mary responded in her comforting voice, "it'll soon be all behind you." Jack didn't respond, and the conversation ended. *She doesn't know how I'm feeling*, he thought. *How could she? I haven't told her.* Fear was a feeling Jack was reluctant to share. As an only child, his immature feelings had been crushed by an overbearing stepmother. He was never quite sure if he was a servant or a slave. One thing he was sure of was that he was not loved as her son. No matter how hard he tried, he could never please her; she would always find fault. She made him feel so useless that he buried his feelings deep and sometimes had to dig deep to find them.

They cleared the lunch things away, and Mary went to have a lie-down; her arthritis was bothering her. She refused to give in to her condition and take her prescribed medication, a decision Jack believed was rooted in obstinacy coupled with a determination to avoid medication addiction. Her question about tomorrow nagged at Jack and caused him to think back to the mishap at the front door earlier. Thresholds, for some reason he kept thinking about thresholds; it was like a recurring dream that he could not decipher—his personal Groundhog Day.

His thoughts migrated to when he was eleven years old. He and his friends had gone to the Saturday afternoon matinee in the cinema to see *Robin Hood and His Merry Men,* after which they immediately set about making their bows and arrows to reenact the skirmishes between Robin Hood and the sheriff of Nottingham in Sherwood Forest. It was during one of their reenactments that Jack looked out from behind a tree and was struck by an arrow just above his right eye. Blood poured down his face; there was much concern and consternation; he was rushed to the doctor. In those days there were no accident and emergency hospital units. He remembered the doctor telling his stepmother he was a very lucky boy; had the arrow hit him a quarter of an inch lower, he would have lost the eye. The fear of losing his eye stayed with Jack from that day on; he bore the physical scar and emotional scars for the rest of his life.

As the afternoon unwound, his thoughts unraveling, he realized that he was actually confronting something he had kept well hidden in the recesses of his mind—the fear of losing his sight. *Now,* he thought, *maybe I am being forced to see things more clearly.*

The countdown for Jack's tomorrow had started about two years previous, but he had not fully understood then that the countdown clock had actually started ticking. He had presented for a routine eye examination with his optician, and everything seemed to be in order. There was no need to change the prescription for his eyeglasses. A couple of months later, Jack experienced some difficulty reading in artificial light. At first he thought it was the old energy-efficient lamp bulbs they were using, so he replaced them with new ones. However, after installing the brightest bulbs he could find, he experienced no significant difference. If anything, it was getting worse. As a last resort, he took to using a headlamp for reading but after a little while that too proved inadequate. Encouraged by Mary, he grasped the nettle and consulted his optician.

The diagnosis this time was not so good; cataracts were developing in his right eye. The prognosis was that the cataracts would ripen over time and that sooner rather than later he would have to have eye surgery to have them removed.

He didn't like the sound of it then and didn't like the thought of it now, especially since he now knew that removing the cataracts meant surgically removing the infected lens from his eye and replacing it with an artificial lens. *No,* he thought, *it was not like a routine visit to the dentist.* He carried the scars from his Robin Hood adventures and saw them every time he looked in the mirror.

He had read the preoperation literature and studied the illustrative diagrams of the eyeball provided by the hospital ophthalmic unit. His procedure would be carried out by an experienced eye surgeon or a supervised trainee. The process of cataract removal required the surgeon to make an incision in the eye, soften the infected lens using ultrasonics, remove it by suction, and implant an artificial lens into the eye to replace the extracted cataract-infected lens. The incision was then stitched up, and hopefully all would be well. Of course he went on to read the information provided on possible complications during and after the operation. That cheered him up no end. Nothing was 100 percent guaranteed; it could go wrong. Why did they only do one eye at a time? Because it could go wrong, and if it did the patient would only have one eye left, or right! The deeply secreted fear reared its ugly head again. The mere thought of someone cutting into his eye filled him with fear and trepidation. It was nothing like a routine visit to the dentist for a checkup, or a replacement filling. No way. In truth, Jack was terrified. It didn't matter what anyone said about how easy or routine the procedure was; his fear could not be subdued; he could not suppress it. But the irony was that although the cataracts had dimmed his vision, in his mind's eye he was seeing things in a completely different light.

Almost two years had passed since his optician had referred him for cataract replacement consideration and one year since he had been placed on the waiting list for surgery. Two years to think about self, in a dance that never ends, like a wheel that never stops spinning. He now realized that the process he had been engaged in was in essence self-deception, a raging fire burning deep within him. It had charred his very soul.

Mary had asked him about tomorrow. Jack now as he sat pondering, resolved that for him from now on there was no tomorrow; there was only today. Today was his tomorrow every day now for the rest of his life. Thresholds he knew went nowhere; they remained in situ; the only in or out was crossing. That's when he decided to confide his fear of losing his sight to Mary.

Tomorrow in calendar time was Thursday. Two days previous, on the Monday afternoon sitting where he was now sitting, he had taken a phone call. It was from the ophthalmic unit of the hospital asking him if he could be ready for eye surgery this coming Thursday. Stunned, Jack could only mumble in disbelief, "This week?"

And so it was that almost two years of waiting had been suddenly reduced to three days. The die was cast; the game was up, and it was tomorrow or never. He could not sidestep it. In an inner space in his mind, Jack had hidden his uncertainty, fear, and dread. Now he had to summon up all his courage to confront them head-on, eyeball to eyeball, and that is what he resolved to do. The eye chosen first for surgery was the one narrowly missed by the arrow when he was eleven playing at being Robin Hood.

In his mind he found another inner space where peace, contentment, self-believe, and courage resided. He let his thoughts dwell and deepen there. Jack's mind was made up. Tomorrow he would walk into the hospital ophthalmic unit for his eye surgery appointment with Mary by his side holding his hand; if not physically, psychologically at least, eyes wide open. After all, "always look forward" was Jack's proclaimed mantra; now all he had to do was live it.

Broken Biscuits

Billy Bell sat at his kitchen table enjoying the morning sun beaming in through the window, eating his breakfast of porridge, tea, and oatcake biscuit. He was in no rush, at peace with himself listening to the music of blackbirds in the tree outside in his back yard. Porridge consumed he broke the biscuit, dipped a piece into his tea, and ate it. As he sat there, memories caressed the corners of his mind.

Rising early, a habit formed in childhood like working a paper route for the local paper shop, as newsagents were then called, had instilled in him a lifelong love for the dawning of every day. The feeling of a whole world, wondrous in its diversity, awakening to birdsong, before the noise of humanity overwhelmed it, he found deeply moving. First footfall printing on an empty street was to him like a step into the unknown. The dawning of the day slowly illuminating empty streets and blinded windowed dwellings fueled his fertile imagination, luring him into realms of childhood fantasy.

All his life Billy had lived in his two up, two down end of terrace kitchen house. Born and reared in it. Today was his seventy-fifth birthday. The youngest of four children, he had a brother, Robert, and two sisters, Mary and Elizabeth. Sadly his mother, father, sisters, and brother were all gone now, passed over, he hoped in faith, to their eternal reward. As he chewed on the last bits of broken biscuit and savored his tea, he thought of his mother kneeling, black leading the small coal-fired range that she had cooked on every day. The kitchen he sat eating in now was no more than a scullery then—no room for a table of any kind.

Getting free coal for the range was no problem. His father was an engine driver on the narrow-gauge railway line that once connected his seaside hometown with towns and villages inland. The trains carried passengers and hauled freight, including wagonloads of imported coal. Young Billy knew the coal train timetables by heart. Once or twice a week he would walk the line, gathering up the spill from the overfilled coal wagons, bagging and taking it home in a little purpose-made four-wheeled pushcart. Coal picking, the locals called it. He was never one for not looking a gift horse in the mouth; it never occurred to him then that he might be stealing.

His gift of free coal would often be welcomed by his mother with a farl of fresh-baked soda bread topped with homemade blackberry jam. Billy, with his brother and sisters, harvested the wild blackberries from hedgerows in the summer, telling themselves they did it for their mother, though often returning home having consumed more than they had gathered. On butter-making day, he would be gifted a cup of fresh buttermilk. On a rare occasion his mother would take down the biscuit tin she kept on the mantelpiece above the range, in anticipation of the unexpected visitor, and offer him a broken biscuit, if there was one, from her cache. Broken biscuits for children and whole biscuits for visitors.

His mother's name was Mary. Mary Anne in full, she was christened Mary, and her given confirmation name was Anne. She was always called Mary Anne. Tradition he supposed given her rural background and the religious customs of the time. He was christened William, and his confirmation name was Thomas, but all he was ever called was Billy. She wasn't very tall, standing only about four feet two inches in her stocking feet. He would have described her as petite. Smiling, he remembered she always wore high-heeled shoes, in fact very high-heeled shoes. He wondered how she could walk in them without tumbling over. By the time he was twelve years old, Billy was taller than his mother. When he looked down on her as she looked up at him, it always felt very strange, odd somehow, not quite right.

Diminutive she might have been, but she was no pushover. Her mind was razor sharp, always ready with an answer for anything, especially anything that roused her ire. One day a neighbor, a stout red-faced woman who had been down to the foot of the street to watch a parade going by, called out to his mother in passing, "Mary Anne, that was as good as my breakfast to me." His mother replied instantly, "Auch, Martha, sure your belly is easily filled; I'll go on in to have mine now," shutting the door behind her, leaving the street to itself and her neighbor with her mouth hanging open like a swinging farmyard gate.

His childhood home was simple enough—two upstairs bedrooms, front and back; downstairs a scullery with cold water tap over a jar box and living room that opened out onto the street. There was a small backyard at the bottom of which was the outside lavatory with a corrugated tin roof and whitewashed walls on the inside. It was a drafty, inhospitable place on a windy winter's night, accessed by torchlight; he shivered at the very thought of it.

It was basic at best all right; he remembered picking off and nibbling on flakes of whitewash from the lavatory walls, wondering if he had had some dietary deficiency or need that made him want to eat lime.

Everyone living on the street then was in the same boat, so to speak, and yet somehow they all seemed contented with their respective lots. His parents managed the sleeping arrangements, in their home very simply—females in one bedroom and males in the other. Not like today, children with their own bedrooms, personal televisions, and smart phones. How on earth did his mother and father ever have the privacy to love each other as man and wife, he had often wondered, with the sort of bedsprings they slept on? He could hear the people next door sometimes tossing and turning trying to get to sleep on a quiet night. Well, that's what he thought then. Billy laughed out loud to himself as the notion eased across the years of memory. Times had changed right enough he acknowledged since he was a child. Rare old times indeed.

Billy was a bachelor. Oh, he had the occasional fling but never experienced the desire to marry, or so he convinced himself. *Strange*, he thought, as his very best friend was a woman, Sadie Crosier, who had lived at the bottom of the street. She had married, married well he had heard remarked; they were childhood friends, and that had always seemed too much to risk. Maybe it was a chance he should have taken, but it was too late now. They kept in touch though. Always good to have a friend to talk to, confide in, when the rivers of life run turbulent.

He had done up the house a few years ago with the help of a council improvement grant. It was comfortable, had a lived in feel about it. The scullery had been replaced with a brand new kitchen; the outside lavatory made way for a new bathroom; central heating replaced his mother's range; no black leading for Billy, oh no, he'd seen enough of that; new double-glazed replacement windows were installed throughout; and thermal insulation was added to the external walls. It was snug, with the luxury, for him, of hot running water when needed for a shower. *Right enough,* he thought. The shower beats the tin bath in front of the range he had used when a child. It wasn't "modern, modern," but it did for him; he was comfortable.

Billy had served his time at the plastering, a tough job in his day. He was a skilled tradesman. A culture of no work no pay pervaded the building trades then. Tough enough for some today on zero hour's contracts, but in his day it was tougher. No minimum or living wage or anything like that then. It was all about survival. Families and communities pulled together, cared for each other, and shared with each other. They knew the difference between the necessities of life and luxuries; they survived on cooperation and credit often referred to as "tick." The "Ticky" man was a common sight up the street on a Friday night collecting his dues when he could find folk in. He well remembered bringing home his first pay packet, feeling proud handing it over to his mother. She was so pleased. "Auch, Billy," she said. "God love you, son; sure you keep something for yourself." His mother taught him to be careful with his pennies, as his occasional girlfriends would observe. From the first day he started work he never failed to put a bit by for the rainy day. Now at seventy-five years of age he had more than enough set aside to cover his funeral costs when his time came to go. The television adverts exhorting the elderly not to burden others with their funeral costs were wasting their time on him. His "exit charge," as he called it, "no need for a passport for that one-way trip," he would often say. A different kind of permit altogether was needed for where he wanted to go. It had to be earned too, but that was a different kind of work altogether.

The sun had moved on from when Billy had awoken to the early-morning birdsong, got up out of bed, and dressed. As always he had somewhere to go, something to do. As a child at home, there was always something to do, some chore or other. His daily routines, rooted in his early-morning paper route, were well established habits now. Billy liked routine. It felt comfortable. It felt safe.

Leaving the house dressed in a pair of brown loafers, tan slacks, matching socks, a baize shirt, and cream-colored jacket, he felt good in himself, not a bother on him. There was life in the old dog yet. He paused in the hall to set the intruder alarm, and it dawned on him for the first time the import of just what it was he was about to do. When he was growing up on this street people left their doors open; there was nothing to be afraid of; they had nothing worth stealing. He was more often in and out of friends' houses than his own. These neighborly comings and goings were the very rhythm of community life. *That was how we were then,* he thought, *how we lived. We knew each other, needed each other; our well-being depended on each other. Times had changed, though.* There was a different wind in the air now. *We are supposed to be better off,* he thought, as he set the intruder alarm and pulled his front door shut tight behind him.

Outside on the footpath he paused, looked down, and noticed the cracked paving slab he was standing on and, smiling, tapped with the toe of his shoe. As children they had invented a game they called broken biscuits. The idea was to try and navigate your way down the footpath on one side of the street and up the other side without stepping on a broken or cracked paving slab. You could hop, skip, or jump, so long as you didn't land on a cracked paving slab. He had never ever tried to count the hours they had spent on this childish pursuit. At least it was exercise—physical and arithmetical. *The ingenuity and resourcefulness of children then was way beyond adult imagination*, he thought, *and still is too.* Childish play, with all its bumps and bruises, has a logic all its own.

The narrow street, as he looked down, was lined with cars, some very expensive cars too. No front gardens here to pave over for car parking. In his day he recalled the milk and coal were delivered to each doorstep by horse and cart. That was the sum total of vehicular traffic. Children played in the street; it was their playground, and they were safe. *Right enough; times really have changed,* he thought. *I hardly know anybody living on the street now*, forgetting of course that today was also his day, his time.

He remembered well all the ones he had lived and grown up with on the street. He was the last of his generation still living there. All the others had passed over, as they say, or had moved on up the social ladder. He could name them all if he had time, but time was moving on.

Billy glanced up to the top of the street to where the big mansion house used to be, but it too was gone, demolished, replaced by a residential care facility. *But no matter*, he thought. *They don't bother me, and I don't bother them.* He could have said, "They don't know me, and I don't know them," thinking, *What's the difference? Was it Sinatra or Acker Bilk who had sung "Strangers on the Shore?" What does it matter anyway? We're all practically strangers now one way and another*, he admitted to himself. What would he have given to see a couple of boys kicking ball on the street again? But not against his gable wall, if you please! *Yes, be very careful what you wish for Billy*, he thought.

The four fifteen-story blocks of flats built in the sixties at the bottom of the street were also long gone. The wrecking ball slung from the end of a huge crane made short work of them. *Thank God for small mercies,* he thought. As he paused at his front door and looked around, he realized for the first time that he could see for miles and miles up the loch shore into the distance, to the hills beyond. *Suppose it's like most folk*, he reasoned, *we look but we don't really see.* It had never occurred to him before that he lived so far above sea level. He thought of the winter past and the poor folk flooded out of their homes, reassured by the notion that it would take a flood of biblical proportions before the water would reach his front door.

As he stood and gazed, the image in his mind's eye changed. It was as if he was looking at a black and white photograph of the old "Co-Op" building with its huge fully glazed front façade that had once stood at the foot of the street when he was a child.

It was always a treat as children to go to the "big Co," as they affectionately called it. Sometimes his older sister Lizzie would take him down with her when she had a penny or two to spend. She would take him in, by the hand, and Lizzie would ask the big man behind the counter for two penny worth of broken biscuits. The big man would fill a brown paper bag with broken biscuits, of all shapes and sizes. Then they would scamper off up home and have a wee party in the house.

Coincidence or not, it was on this very day sixty-five years ago on his tenth birthday that Billy had earned himself a couple of pennies from his early-morning paper route. So feeling flush and grown up, he headed down to the "big Co." A wee bit apprehensively he approached the counter as he had done with his big sister Lizzie before. His nose barely reached the top of the counter as he peered up; the big man was there. Hesitantly he said, "Two penny worth of broken biscuits, please, sir." The big man looked down on him for a moment or two and then said, "Sorry, son, we don't have any broken biscuits today." Billy remembered exactly how he felt at that moment. It was etched into the very fiber of his being. His wee face fell; it looked like it could hold a week's rain; his top lip trembled; his shoulders dropped in disappointment, and his eyes misted up. After a moment's hesitation he lowered his eyes and without a word turned sheepishly to go. The big man behind the counter, sensing Billy's distress, leaned over the counter, put his hand gently on Billy's shoulder, and whispered in his ear, "Hold a wee minute, son, and I'll break some for you."

Billy waited in quiet anxious anticipation barely able to breathe until the big man reached over the counter and handed down to him a brown paper bag full of broken biscuits in exchange for his tuppence. Trembling with inner excitement, he walked tall out of the "big Co" that day clutching the bag of broken biscuits tightly to his chest and ran home as fast as he could to share his treasure with his family. It was a day he would never ever forget.

Billy blinked, and the vision of the "Co-Op" at the foot of the street disappeared. Strange, he thought, that that act of kindness of the big man behind the counter in the Co-Op, breaking the biscuits, especially for him, and calling him son, sixty-five years ago—a lifetime ago—could be recalled with such vivid intensity.

Memories, he thought, but he was lingering, time was passing, and he had somewhere to go. At the bottom of the street he paused noting that the barbers' shop too was gone as was the family butchers. All demolished in the name of progress. Perhaps it was all for the good.

Turning left, he walked past the recently opened new library building; it was a journey he made every day. Climbing the short incline past the old red brick Carnegie library, now a museum, he paused briefly to catch his breath. It was a place of fond memories for him. A place as a child he would enter without hesitation to find his quiet space. Now a museum, where things were put on display. *Difficult to display memories and feelings*, he thought, as he crossed the road and made his way toward the old labor exchange building. He walked on past it, the "Bru," as it was known affectionately by his generation, now a beauty salon, but as he recalled there was no beauty or dignity in being unemployed. *There must be some irony in that*, he thought, racking his brains but coming up blank. Then he heard the chapel bell began to toll, bringing him back to the present as it summoned the faithful to morning mass.

Minutes later he entered the chapel as he had always done through the middle door, blessed himself with the holy water in the font in the porch, paused, and gathered himself together before going in. Inside he turned toward the altar, bowed his head, and took a pew. It was the same pew in which he had sat every Sunday, with his mother and father, brother and sisters.

Kneeling he began the process of examining his conscience, an examination of a lifelong conscience. It struck him as a bit strange that the older he got the more he focused on the minutiae of his recollected childhood misdemeanors. In the end, when he had finished, he found, as he always did, that he was more concerned about what he had not done than about what he had done.

His meditation was interrupted when the priest entered from the sacristy, acknowledged the altar, turned toward the handful of senior citizens making up the congregation and began the morning mass. Billy missed the Latin mass, especially the sung Latin mass; he could still sing it and recite the prayers in Latin too, but he was not a traditionalist. His religious education, which began when dangling on his mother's knee, developed further when his formal schooling started in the primary school that was next door to the church. He became an altar boy until he left school at the age of fourteen. The school was gone now, demolished to make way for a car park.

As the priest progressed through the preliminaries of the mass toward its climax, Billy's attentiveness increased. He always tried to place himself in the presence of Jesus, in the upper room at the last supper in Jerusalem over two millennium ago, as the priest raised the communion bread, broke it, and spoke the words of consecration. The chapel seemed stilled in reverent anticipation. The moment was extraordinary. No matter his doubts, his concerns, he knew his faith was unshakable. Billy was a Christian because he chose to be a Christian.

Then Billy's mind flashed back to that summer morning when on his tenth birthday sixty-five years ago, the big man behind the Co-Op counter whispered in his ear, broke the biscuits specially for him, handed them to him, and called him son. It was, he now understood, a blessing on his journey through life. He wondered if, when his big sister Lizzie first took him by the hand into the "big Co" to buy broken biscuits, she was feeling a wee bit apprehensive too and needed him for support. Deeply moved, he recalled that special moment. Life is a journey, he had heard people say, wondering what they really meant. *Right enough,* he thought, but it had taken him almost a lifetime to understand the significance of that simple but profound statement.

When the mass was ended and the priest's blessing given, Billy sat on in the silent chapel pondering the elevation of the breaking of bread, from an everyday occurrence to an act of reparation, sufficient for the salvation of the whole world. His mind turned to the gospel he had just heard read; the beatitudes had troubled Billy all his adult life: "happy are you who are hungry now; you shall be satisfied" and "the meek shall inherit the earth." Slowly over time he had come to realize that his understanding had been too narrow; there were other dimensions to feeding the hungry to explore. He hadn't thought much about social injustice when he was younger, but he did now—couldn't help it—it was everywhere he looked. *People all around are continuously searching hungrily for meaning in their lives,* he thought. His church was offering meditation and silent retreats. Others found peace and a sense of connectedness through yoga and mindfulness. The hungry, he now understood, all of the hungry, including the spiritually hungry, would only be satisfied when they entered the kingdom of God. *Well,* he thought, *each in our own way make that journey incrementally.* A drop in the ocean perhaps, but many drops can make an ocean. *How vast,* he thought, *must be the patience of God to depend on human beings to bring to fruition the Lord's Prayer*—"Your kingdom come on earth as it is in heaven." *Your kingdom come in me too*, he earnestly prayed.

Finally at peace in himself, Billy left the cool, quiet chapel to enjoy the midmorning summer sun. He headed down toward the Main Street. The new oatmeal-colored pavement stretched out before him, sparkling in the bright sunshine. He viewed the growing pavement café culture with vicarious pleasure, thinking that his little market town was becoming more and more European. The only blight, however, was the ever-increasing number of charity shops that in his view was changing the character of the town center, once vibrant but now at best dreary. Almost immediately he chastised himself—happy are the poor; theirs is the kingdom of heaven, but not on my main street, more food for thought. But thinking positively, he conceded that it was a form of recycling, in support of good causes.

Sufficiently self-admonished, he settled into a seat shaded from the sun at a pavement bistro table. When the waitress came, he ordered an espresso and his childhood biscuit of choice—a wagon wheel. *Might as well go the whole hog,* he thought.

When his coffee and wagon wheel arrived, he was a little bemused. The wagon wheel wrapping looked big, but the biscuit inside it felt very small. It was no illusion. When he unwrapped and extracted the wagon wheel, he thought it must have come off of a very small wagon. Just another sign of the downsizing times we live in and how not to feed the hungry.

As he sat there he thought of his mother's tin of biscuits, big man in the "Co-Op" breaking the biscuits for him and calling him son, and the priest at mass breaking the bread, as the son of God asked his disciples to do, and share in memory of him, for the salvation of the world. Without thinking Billy lifted up his chocolate-coated biscuit and broke it, calling to mind the words his late mother would often have said: "Thank God for this day and all that is in it."

Then he sat back, nibbled the broken biscuit, sipped his coffee and people-watched contentedly his morning away. Over his second espresso he kept a watchful eye on the bus stop across the street. When a queue started to form he crossed over and joined it, exchanging words of greeting with folk he knew. Some were carrying bunches of flowers. They were going to spend the afternoon in the cemetery too, remembering, communing with their saints.

He always spent his birthdays and other special days there.

Forgiving Is Easy

She was home alone when she felt the needle-sharp pain searing her side. Her hand, as if it had a mind of its own, pressed hard against her skin to ease it, but it was not for easing, just like the stitch she sometimes endured when jogging but much more intense. She gritted her teeth hoping it would pass and carried on with what she was doing. She was hanging out the washing, lifting a heavy wet blanket and stretching to lob it over the clothesline, when an excruciating stab of pain brought her crumbling to her knees. Gasping, she knelt on the grass, tears in her eyes unable to move, helpless. Eventually willing herself to move, she gathered up the wet blanket and made her way, crab-like, back into the house and collapsed onto the floor.

It was half past four in the afternoon; her three daughters arrived home from college as usual, dumped their gear in the hallway, and made their way to the kitchen expecting their mother waiting, snacks readied.

She wasn't there; no snacks were readied and no explanatory note for her absence. Thinking she might be resting, they went upstairs and looked in her bedroom; she wasn't there. They looked in the other bedrooms, the living room, and sitting room; she was nowhere to be found. It was unusual but nothing untoward. Their mother often visited friends, resident in a local care home, and frequently lost track of time. From past experience they knew that the care home residents had their evening meal around five o'clock, so if their mother was visiting there she would be home shortly. No worries.

They made tea, set the table for dinner, chatted, and patiently waited. Half past five came and went; their mother had not appeared. They called her on her mobile phone only to hear it ringing out beside the bread bin where she'd left it. This was par for the course, as they say; their mother was, apart from household equipment such as washing machines, technologically challenged; besides she'd often told them she had little use for a mobile phone.

Mary, the youngest of the three, besmudged from afternoon hockey practice, bagged first use of the shower. Sports bag in hand, she made her way to the utility room to load her muddied hockey gear into the washing machine. The utility room door was a little bit reluctant to open, so she gave it a good shove. It yielded so readily that she stumbled in through it over the top of her mother lying spread-eagled, like a bundle of wet washing, on the cold tiled floor. She yelled, "She's here! She's here!"

Her sisters, rushing in response to her yelling, almost fell over her as she crouched beside their mother. The middle sister, Molly, shouted to no one in particular: "What's happened? What's happened?" Mary's anxious eyes appealed to Maggie. "What'll we do? What'll we do?"

Maggie, a final year student, was a trained first aider. She took control of the situation, sending Mary to get a pillow and duvet or blankets to make their mother comfortable, distracting her attention in the process from the sight of their mother lying spread-eagled on the floor. Molly she sent to get water to give her mother to drink if she needed it. Then kneeling, she gently turned her mother's face up so that she could see her full frontal. The face she looked down on was ashen; her skin felt cold; beads of cold sweat freckled her mother's brow, but she was conscious. Her lips were not blue, her face was not drooping, and her arms and hands were clenched around her stomach. She was breathing—short shallow pants—her airways were clear. "Can you hear me, Mummy?" Maggie asked. A slight head nod acknowledged her question. "Who am I?" Maggie said. Through clenched teeth, her mother grunted, "Maggie." When Mary arrived with a duvet and pillow, Maggie made their mother as comfortable as she could, glad she didn't have to use the resuscitation techniques learned in training.

Slowly, with some difficulty, their mother told them what had happened. Maggie intently focused on the here and now; seeing she was still in considerable pain, Maggie wondered what to do next. She wasn't sure if it was safe to try to move her. As far as she could tell by looking and feeling, her mother hadn't broken any bones; her heart seemed okay. Uncertain about what to do and forgetting the time, she rang their doctor. The surgery was closed; it had gone five o'clock. In her anxiety and haste, Maggie didn't jot down the emergency number the surgery's answer machine had spewed out, so, armed with pen and paper, and with increasing anxiety, she rang the surgery again, noted the emergency number given, and made the call. She spoke to someone—explained the situation, described how they had found their mother, the condition she was in and their concerns for her well-being, and answered questions put to her. The call ended with the assurance that the information she provided would be passed on immediately to a nurse or doctor who would get back to them directly.

When Maggie returned to the utility room, her mother was lying with her shoulders propped up against the dishwasher. Somehow she had managed, despite Mary and Molly's concerns, to pull herself up by clutching onto the door of the washing machine. Seeing that she had managed unaided to get into that position Maggie fetched a chair from the kitchen and with her sisters performed a three-person lift, set her securely and comfortably onto it, and carried her into the more hospitable living room. Then they eased her onto the sofa and made her comfortable.

Time eased away unnoticed; her mother's condition if anything was getting worse. Their father was abroad on business and wouldn't be home until the following morning; he was probably in the air somewhere; nothing he could do anyway. Having done everything they could they waited, but worry gnawed at them. Suddenly the phone rang, stridently shattering the silence that nurtured their anxiety. The caller, a nurse, confirmed the information Maggie had already provided, inquired if there was any change in their mother's condition, advised them to keep her warm and hydrated, and informed them that he would contact a doctor who would call them, and with that the terse conversation ended.

Maggie, dead phone in hand, pondered what the nurse had advised but knew that they were doing all that anyway and that what they really needed was expert help now. Frustrated, she cradled the phone. Time drained away, like water dribbling from a tap that badly needed a new washer. Their mother's pain had definitely increased in intensity and spasm frequency.

Should they wait for the doctor to call? How long should they wait? Should they just take the bull by the horns and dial 999 for an ambulance? That was the dilemma they wrestled with until desperation forced Maggie to run next door for help.

Robert, Uncle Bob they called him when they were children, a silver-haired widower, answered Maggie's urgent banging on his front door. The anxiety on Maggie's face told him all he needed to know before she even spoke; he followed her back to her mother's side. *The pain could be appendicitis*, he thought, but he couldn't be sure and didn't know what to do if it was anyway. But he knew if her appendix ruptured it could be fatal; there was no point in waiting. They lived in a rural area; it could take an ambulance at least half an hour to reach them if one was available and more than a half hour to reach the nearest hospital depending on traffic. The sensible thing to do was to get their mother to the nearest hospital accident and emergency department as soon as possible; "we're taking her to the nearest A@E now," he said, and with that went to bring his car round to their front door. They chaired-lifted their mother out to the car and bundled, duvet wrapped, into the back seat and set off for the nearest A@E some thirty miles away. Maggie sat up front with Bob, her sisters in the back seat with their mother.

At the A&E, their mother was triaged, eventually examined by a doctor, and subjected to various tests resulting in a diagnosis of severe gallstones. The preferred treatment regime was to try and dissolve the offending stones before considering anything more invasive. With that her mother was made comfortable, supplied with appropriate medication, and discharged. Some eight hours after arriving at the A&E, they departed for home bone weary but relieved. When they did get home the sky was brightening; it had gone three o'clock in the morning, the street was eerily quiet, and their morning milk had not been delivered. It wasn't long after they put their mother to bed that the want of sleep forced them to their beds too. Robert said good night, even though it was morning, and went home saying he would look in later.

When the sun had risen in its daily quest to blanket out the night, Maggie, unraveling from her sleep, realized that she had forgotten to set her alarm clock and had overslept. In great haste she dressed, gathered up all her stuff, and ran up the road to catch her seven thirty bus to college only to glimpse the back end of it disappearing out of sight. She had missed it. Distraught tears wetted her eyes as she walked back home. Today, the day she had worked so hard toward, was disappearing out of sight. Her first A-level examination was scheduled for half past nine, and she had missed the bus.

Closing the door quietly as she reentered the house, Maggie met her mother inching her way slowly down the stairs, concern, not the pain of yesterday, etched on her face. She knew Maggie had missed the bus; the work she had put in in preparation for her A-level exams, and how upset she must be. At the bottom of the stairs she held Maggie close, hugged her tight, and comforted her with whispered assurances that everything would be all right.

One of Maggie's teachers living nearby left home in the morning for work at around eight fifteen. Without a second thought Maggie's mother unearthed the teacher's home phone number and called him, confident that when the drama of the night before was explained and the consequences for Maggie missing her bus, her plea on behalf of her daughter for a lift to college this once would find a sympathetic ear. It did; the only problem was the teacher explained that he was car sharing with another teacher, and she was collecting him today. However, he was confident that there won't be any problem and that they would call for Maggie around eight fifteen.

Eight fifteen came and went. Anxious, she rang the teacher again only to be informed that he had left for college some time ago. She was frantically thumbing through the telephone directory hopefully searching for an available taxi when their front door bell chimed. Maggie attended to the door, returning moments later with Robert from next door. Sensing that something was amiss, he sat on the sofa beside Maggie's mother. "What on earth's wrong, Nora?" he said, and that's when the floodgates of pent-up anxiety, frustration, and desperation opened and vented real, raw, and raging. He held her until she quieted and calmed, and then he told Maggie to gather what she needed for college; they would leave immediately. On the way out he asked about the other girls. Nora brightening said, "Let them sleep," and with that Maggie was on her way to her exam appointment.

Later, crises averted, she gathered herself together, remembered to take her medication, and settled down to a soothing cup of tea when the phone rang; it was her husband Frank. He was at the airport and would be home in an hour depending on traffic. She smiled as she put the phone down knowing he would arrive with gifts for them all, and she would unload on him all the happenings in his absence. Mary and Molly surfaced midmorning unaware of Maggie's dilemma earlier and busied themselves filling the house with smells of freshly baked breads and tart-de-tan.

Over dinner with their neighbor Robert, they waded through the events of the past forty-eight hours. On the positive side, she was feeling much better; her pain had eased, Frank was home, and Maggie had sat her exam. When asked how she got on, Maggie just said she thought she had done all right, which interpreted usually means "I think I've done well." Nora was content all was well on the home front. She was saying goodnight to Robert with a grateful hug when Frank produced from his duty-free bag a vintage cognac. "I bought this to keep for a special occasion," he said, "and I think this is it." When appropriate glasses were produced, he poured a generous measure for Robert, a wee drop for himself, and a taste for Nora. The girls had to make do with fruit juice. Raising his glass, Frank toasted good neighbors. When Nora and the girls had gone to bed, Frank and Robert had a bit more cognac and together caressed the dawning.

Nora's stomach pain eased as the gallstones dissolved away into distant memory, her all clear prognosis gratefully received. Family life slipped quietly back into its cycle of routine activities that filled their days, spiced with the seasonal pursuits they pursued. All was well or so it seemed. Although Nora's stomach pain had disappeared, a wriggling worm of agitation was growing in her mind. On several occasions after the morning drama of getting Maggie to college for her first A level, Nora, as chance would have it, bumped into the teacher whom she had in desperation turned to for help. They small-talked about this and that—the weather, the price of vegetables, everything under the sun—all the while tiptoeing around the issue that was worming in Nora's mind. These mundane sterile encounters continued for weeks; the worm in Nora's head grew longer, stronger, and more agitated.

At first she felt confused. She rewound that morning over and over again in her head. Had she missed something? She couldn't understand what had happened; her mind a whirlpool of confused thoughts, had she done something wrong? She didn't know what to do to satisfy the wriggling demon growing inside her head. As her confusion festered, it morphed into hurt and then raging resentment. All she had asked for in her desperate need was help. Was it too much to ask? She felt let down in her moment of need by someone she trusted to care for her child. Everything she had been brought up to believe and practice had been destroyed that fateful morning. But being the person she was, she chided herself. Was she just being scrupulous, oversensitive, too judgmental? She talked it through with Frank endlessly, monotonously, over and over again. His advice was unchanging: ignore it, put it behind you, it's not worth it, pull yourself together, move on, they are not worth it, and people treat you like shit anyway. *Maybe you're right,* she thought, *but that doesn't satisfy the wriggling worm in my head.* She felt like a mushroom searching desperately for a chink of light while something was nibbling away her peace of mind.

One glorious spring morning, feeling totally unencumbered, she went for a walk—a kind of meditation walk—feeling her way and embracing everything larger than herself. Her wanderings took her along the seafront close to home but in a different direction than usual. Eventually she found herself in a small cove where little fishing boats gently bobbed in sympathy with the motion of the ebbing tide. All the paraphernalia of fishing littered the high water mark; lobster pots, fishing tackle, and nets hung up to dry in the gentle onshore breeze. She sat for a while on a bench at peace with herself and everything around her. It was indeed a glorious morning—the soft caressing sun and gentle breeze, inducing a welcome feeling of well-being. Sitting looking at nothing in particular, she realized she was actually gazing through a fisherman's net wafting in the breeze, her view beyond a framed networked sea and landscape montage. At that moment she remembered something Maggie had talked about preparing for her A-level psychology exam; the brain was a network of nodes and links, just like the fishing net she was looking through. She laughed out loud, a spontaneous release of emotional tension; her mushroom had found its chink of light. Pondering the notion it occurred to her that each cell in her emotional network was full of little mushrooms scrambling toward a keyhole of light. It was exactly how she felt. Thinking about getting back home, she shifted her gaze to fully visually explore the little cove.

That's when she saw the old man sitting, fishing net spread out across his lap patiently knot by knot and link by link untangling his tangled net. He had a little boy helping him, probably a grandson, she thought. Engrossed in his task, he didn't see her observing him. As he worked to untangle the net, the little boy would draw it out away from him. It was slow, patient work; damaged knots and links would be renewed until the net was fit for purpose again. That's what Nora at that moment resolved to do, unravel the tangled net of feelings and emotions in her head to make herself in every respect fit for purpose again. To begin the process of unraveling her emotional net, she had to start with the root cause.

Nora couldn't wait for an opportunity to bump into the teacher from up the road again, only this time serendipity was replaced by intent. After the usual exchange of pleasantries, Nora suggested coffee in the coffee shop she knew the teacher favored, knowing full well it would be difficult for him to refuse. It was a win-win situation for Nora, not that she took any pleasure in it, engineered as it was. They small-talked for a little, and then Nora asked if he would care to enlighten her as to what actually happened the morning her daughter's promised lift to college failed to materialize.

The teacher's explanation, it turned out, was perfectly simple; his senior colleague he was car sharing with that day chose not to give her daughter a lift because she didn't want to set a bad example. Nora smiling benignly said, "Thank you. I understand now; that explains it," and changed the conversation. A little later she excused herself and left the teacher to himself and his coffee. Walking home mulling over her meeting, Nora thought, *I was ill; my daughter was in need; you and your colleague without a second thought abandoned us. I couldn't do that to a dog; you had your mobile phone with you, so you could have phoned and told me; you've had many opportunities since and didn't and probably wouldn't have mentioned it, if I had not dragged it out of you today.* As she walked and thought, Nora's pace quickened. She felt light on her feet as if a huge oppressive load had been lifted off her back. If she had a skipping rope she would have skipped all the way home; she felt that good. Her tangled net was unraveling.

Later that day her thoughts turned to the car driver, the senior colleague the teacher had sheltered behind. *It wasn't his decision, oh no, it was hers! She's the culprit.* Nora knew her and her family well; they were reared, as they say, on the same street. She was an only child, bubble-wrapped, cosseted, and shaped under her mother's apron—never allowed to play on the street with other children, didn't know the fun and lasting friendships fostered in childish games. She was shepherded with her mother's clinging hand to and from school every day. Later she traveled every day to teacher training college from home, eventually emerging as a fully fledged teacher, fit for the purpose of shaping others. The irony of it tickled her lips as she thought about it. *How absurd*, she thought, *that this virgin of real world life experiences could bring any added value to book learning in a classroom.*

Nora focused on why she didn't help Maggie that morning. The why was important; she didn't want to set a bad example! It was clear now to Nora, another bit of unraveling done; she thought she was behaving in an exemplary manner—in a good and caring way that other people should follow! She was the good example setter. *Is that it?* Nora thought. *It's as simple as that! It's a good example to abandon someone in need and bad example to help someone in need. What a pillock*, she thought. Nora knew from leafing through Maggie's psychology notes that several things shape people and influence behaviors, and top of the list was family.

Years later when her children had left college, negotiated university, found worthwhile jobs, and chose not to practice their Christian faith, she asked them why. It was all rooted, it turned out, in the day her daughter, because her mother had taken ill, missed her bus to college. Teachers don't practice what they preach, her children told her. *It's not often that the effect of a specific behavior can be attributed with certainty; another conundrum sorted,* she thought.

Nora wondered what the example giver would say to that! *Example*, she thought, *is a dual carriageway, the giver and the receiver moving in different directions, sometimes the receiver giving more than the giver. It's a bit like listening; often the listener is giving much more than the speaker.*

Her net was almost completely unraveled; she had only one more knot to undo. The final knot loosened a little in church one Sunday. The car driver that long ago fateful day, now a minister of the word, read the story about the Good Samaritan. She observed her closely as she left her pew and paraded to the lectern, fussily repositioned the Bible, adjusted the microphone, put on her designer eyeglasses, and surveyed the congregation. She spoke the words robotically, clearly, precisely without feeling, expression, or phrasing. Nora wondered if she even understood the message embedded within the text she was reading and if the thought ever crossed her mind that perhaps the Good Samaritan was giving bad example! *A lifetime of teaching, and so little learned,* she thought.

The last knot was almost undone. *Forgiving is the easy bit*, she thought. *It's the forgetting that's the bugger.* Perhaps had she dealt with it differently at the time instead of letting it fester silently deep within her inner self, she might have moved on sooner. She could have asked her daughter's teacher sooner what had happened, heard his explanation, cleared the air, and openly expressed her disappointment, but she hadn't. If she had had the courage to act differently at the time, it would have been better all round. With that thought, the last knot was undone; the tangled net in her mind was fully unraveled.

She had learned her lesson, rid herself of the worm of resentment until the next time her mind entangled itself in the process of being. *That's what we do in life,* she thought *unravel the tangled emotional networks in our heads once we get past the blame game.*

She did find some use for her mobile phone, though, a handy thing to have from time to time. She always has it with her now, and she learned to appreciate the wonders of it, without developing an addiction.

Hands Tell All

His morning's work in the garden finished, Bobby Baxter sat contentedly under a blossoming apple tree. His grimy clasped hands rested on his stomach. Hard physical work in his younger days kept his belly flat and firm, not body sculpting in expensive gyms. The interlocking fingers of his hands were gnarled, lumpy, twisted, and knotted, like the tangled branches of the corkscrew hazel tree he was looking at, his fingernails covered with dried clotted garden soil.

Looking at his hands, he wondered how someone gifted in the art of palmistry would interpret them. He knew some of the basics. The left hand allegedly showed potential, a bit too late for him, and the right showed how that potential would be realized. In palmistry there were, he knew, four major types of hands: earth hands associated with practicality and levelheadedness, air hands associated with intellectualism and curiosity, water hands associated with artistic ability and emotionality, and fire hands associated with energy and dynamism. He was looking down on the back of his hands; palmists looked at the soft underbelly of the hands searching for the heart, head, life, and fate lines to distill some germ of substance on which to base an interpretation. He unclasped his hands, held his palms facing upward, looked at them again, and wondered what the panelists on the *What's My Line* television program of yesteryear would have made of them.

How many times had he raised these hands in prayer, making the sign of the cross? How many times had these hands been raised in thanksgiving for his children and all the blessings bestowed upon them? How many times had these hands admonished his children? Had these hands lost forever their caressing touch? Hands on the ends of outstretched arms he knew could be compelling instruments of expression: loving, calming, reasoning, inviting, entreating, welcoming, comforting, encouraging openness and trust. Folded arms concealing hands could mean don't disturb, private, or guarded.

Enough he thought he grew up with his hands, or they grew up with him. He didn't invent them; evolution took care of all that. They were just there taken for granted.

At school he wasn't much of a student; it just wasn't interesting enough to lure him away from football. He had lived to regret that.

When he left school at the ripe old age of fourteen, he did what most working-class boys did back then. He dutifully followed in his father's footsteps to embrace manhood by serving out a bricklaying apprenticeship with a local building contractor. On his first day on the job, he followed behind his father into the builder's yard, climbed into the back of the cigarette-smoke-filled Bedford van, squeezed into a place between joiners, plasterers, and bricklayers already boarded, and readied to go to a building site some thirty miles away. He spent the first week learning how to make unsmoked drinkable tea in billycans over wood-burning fires. With his first week's wages he bought himself a trowel and a wooden three-foot folding rule—a rule not a ruler. The trowel he bought had a long steel flat spear-shaped blade with sharp edges. Today he thought it could easily have been classed as an offensive weapon. It had a leather-bound raised handle, which he later learned how to shape to give better lift.

The building they were working on was surrounded by scaffolding at first-floor level. On his second week on the job he was allowed to climb up unto it, and within a very short time he became an expert scaffold walker. His job up there, however, was to keep the mortar on the mortarboards placed at intervals along the scaffold fit for use—stop it from drying out or stiffening up, keeping it elastic enough for spreading along the wall being built brick by brick course by course. That was how he began to learn and develop his trowel skills. Bucket of water in his left hand, trowel in his right hand, scraping and slurring the mortar, troweling and retroweling until it was fit for purpose, his right wrist aching at close of day. He keenly observed how the old hands used their trowels to shape and then lift a large wedge of mortar and with a flick of the wrist spread it without loss along the top of the course of bricks, pucker it with the tip of the trowel, and remove the surplus mortar from the face of the bricks with the trowel's sharp edge to receive the next course of bricks. It was poetry in motion to him, and he practiced it as he attended to his duties husbanding the mortarboards day after day.

In the beginning he didn't know that mortar burned into flesh and caused finger hacks and sores that were difficult to heal, but he found out, like most things in the building trade, the hard way. The sides of his index finger and thumb of his right hand gripping the trowel handle were raw and damson stained with tacky blood. The soft silk like skin cover over the knuckles on his fingers where they brushed against the glutinous mortar he mixed and remixed crazed, hacked, and wept blood that congealed and flowed in rhythm with the movement with his hand. He also discovered some of the handed-down preventative and healing remedies like soaking hands in brine and urine.

Came the day when he was deemed ready by his mentor brickie to "join the line" building a wall. He was made up. He took to it like a duck to water. It was his third week on the line when he had his first mishap. Tapping a reluctant brick into place in its bed of mortar with the edge of his sharp trowel, he tapped too hard—not on the brick but on the nail of his index finger of his left hand. Needless to say, he lost the nail and couldn't pick his nose with that finger for weeks. Tentative at first, he soon mastered the knack of picking up the bricks with his left hand spinning and twirling them around to present them as they should be laid into the bed of mortar on the wall being built.

Rough bricks and soft skin were not ideally matched, he soon discovered. Abrasive contact between the fingers of his left hand and the rough bricks and concrete blocks wore away the soft skin covering his fingers. It was one evening at home when he reached for a cup of tea and couldn't hold it because it felt so hot that he realized that the skin on his fingers was so smooth he doubted he could have left traceable fingerprints on the cup. The next day the fingertips of his left hand were raw, bleeding, and sore. With fingers wrapped up in black insulating tape, looking like roses begging for deadheading, he persevered, a wounded, obstinate trowel wielder learning his trade.

He searched for and found books on the craft of bricklaying in the local library, learned about different kinds of bonds—English bond and Flemish bond, the building of arches—and asked questions for which some experienced old hands had no answers. After completing his apprenticeship, getting married, and starting a family, he renovated their first home and then later built their new home himself on a superb site overlooking the sea. Still there was a yearning inside him. Laying bricks and building a house was not challenging enough; it didn't stretch him. It was a wet winter's morning with gusting rain and chilling winds when working high up on a scaffold, building a factory chimney, he saw a farmer cross the fields below him take his cattle in out of the weather. That was the moment when he questioned what he was doing and, more importantly, whether it was what he really wanted to do for the rest of his working life. By the time he had climbed back down from the scaffold to ground level, he knew the answer and the direction he would take.

Given his background, he had to start at the bottom. He enrolled in night classes at the local technical college and two years later passed his City & Guilds craft examinations. That was only the start; now his appetite for learning was whetted. He enrolled in a part-time polytechnic degree course and graduated four years later with honors. Then an opportunity presented itself that he could not refuse; he applied for and was successful in landing a job as a building control officer in a local authority. He was off the scaffold at last—liberated but still connected to the building industry as a technologist with a scientific leaning.

His new job fascinated him, made him read more around issues, research more in pursuit of knowledge, recognize how much more there was to know, and think about how best to augment the little knowledge he had. He searched around the university websites and eventually found a course that was right up his street, an MSc course in his chosen discipline offered on a two-year block release mode. It would require approvals, adjustments, and generosity at home and work, but successful completion would bring rewards to all. The two years passed quickly but not easily for him. It was hard, demanding work, and he felt that he was in at the deep end. He was the only mature part-time student enrolled in the course; the other students had honors degrees in the subject they were now taking at a master's level. He had to keep up, and he did. Two years after enrolling in the course, he graduated with all his family there to celebrate the occasion.

Several years seemed to slip by at work, during which he earned several promotions. He was a hands-on person keenly involved in the day-to-day work with his colleagues. Helping, assisting, and advising but never interfering, always available when there was a problem on the table to be addressed. That was the part of the job he loved and at which he excelled. He had long ago realized that building regulations were drafted by lawyers in language often described as legalese, which unfortunately often obscured their real purpose—the design and construction of safe buildings. He was wrestling with one such problem, trying to distill the actual intent of a particular building regulation, when he took a phone call from a friend advising of a vacant post the university was seeking to fill that perhaps he might consider applying for. He read the job description, thought about it, applied, and, as it turned out, was after a round of interviews appointed as a university lecturer.

A university lecturer! He couldn't believe it; free to go to the library to read and study, he was on the proverbial pig's back. He was assigned classes to teach that he relished, was encouraged to research and publish and to apply for and obtain research grants to further his work, and was able to travel abroad and network. He loved it; work was fun. He was a completely different scaffold walker now; he was on a high wire. The day arrived when he presented for his PhD Viva before a panel of eminent professors whose work he had read and drawn from and who had influenced his direction of travel. In the toilet before the Viva, he was sick with nerves. After some six hours of interrogation, discussion, and debate, he was awarded his PhD. At the graduation ceremony, the chancellor of the university conferred the awards by doffing the recipients on the head with his mortarboard. He remembered that day with pride.

He looked at his hands again, reverently rubbed them gently together, and sighed. In a relatively short time, it seemed to him, he was elevated to the top of his profession—a professor. It was an honor and a title he carried easily through the rest of his working life.

As fate would have it, he was supervising two PhD students who were working on projects investigating the behavior of masonry exposed to fire in buildings. To progress their work they needed to build brick wall panels to instrument and test. They discussed their proposed experiments with him in detail, expressing their concerns about getting the brick panels built. They had to be built to reflect reality (i.e., how brick walls were actually built in the real world). They needed three panels five meters long by three meters high. Neither they nor any of the laboratory technicians could build the brick panels, and they were on a tight budget. To get around the problem, he offered the students a deal; he would build them their panels in his spare time if they would help him do it. He smiled as he remembered the looks on their faces. But they accepted his offer. Two weeks later on a Saturday morning, they met in the engineering labs. He started up the electric-powered cement mixer and shoveled in the sand and cement in the optimum proportions, adding water occasionally to show them how to produce a very workable mortar, and then he showed them where he wanted the bricks piled up either side of the mortarboard before he set to work.

Technicians from adjoining labs and other PhD students swelled the initial group to witness what was happening. From an old tattered khaki bag he pulled out a trowel—his old trowel, long thought redundant. *It isn't as big as when new. Its edges have lost their sharpness; its shiny newness has gone too; but it is still usable—a bit like me,* he thought. With elbow grease and a ball of steel wool, he restored its shininess. It would slither and slather with ease through the gungy mortar. A search of the old khaki bag offered up another necessary tool, his old brick hammer. The students barrowed the mortar over to the rigs they had erected to receive the wall panels so that when built and cured they could be fitted as a wall, completing the large furnace enclosure ready for testing.

The lab was filling up with people standing around; they hadn't seen the like of it before and didn't know what to make of it. His hands, now soft from pen pushing, he covered with tight-fitting fabric gloves. He was nothing if not a quick learner and set to work building the panels, installing the instrumentation as directed by his students. He was enjoying himself. At the end of the day, wall panels built, he took the trowel and hurled it like a knife thrower into the mortarboard, where its pointed end stuck, the blade and handle quivering in celebration of a job well done. The cement mixer washed out, trowel cleaned and back in the bag, he stripped off the gloves, put them in the waste bin, shook hands with his students, heaved the old khaki bag onto his shoulder, left the lab, and invited his laborers for a well-earned pint. On his way home he enjoyed a quiet smile.

Retirement was a big decision for him, but in the end it was the right thing to do. He had helped his wife raise seven children to adulthood; it was time for him to give something back to her—time for them to be more together again. Decision made, it was hard to go, but he knew that when he walked out through university gates he would never look back. No point in that; always look forward was his abiding mantra, and so he did. Two years before his retirement, the university had conferred on him the title emeritus professor. At the time he wondered what to do with it. Now he knew. Every so often they would take him down from the shelf of retirement, dust him off, and parade him at two or three public gatherings a year. He didn't mind, especially if the occasions were celebrations of students' work. As retirement time stretched, his university network shrank; there were fewer and fewer familiar faces at these gatherings. He used to be a person of some importance in the university, but those days were now long gone. Maybe he should call it a day.

All that seemed a long time ago. He looked down at his feet, and lying there was his old faithful trowel—now the gardener's preferred tool. It was stained with garden soil, as were his hands and fingernails. Both he and the trowel had lost their shine and sharp edges. Steel wool would bring back the trowel blade's shininess, but it couldn't put a shine on him. He could still lay bricks all right at a much slower rate; his back would give in too soon. Those days were long gone. The good news was he could still wield a pen and work the keys on his laptop, and his mind was clear.

He looked at his hands again and examined them one at a time, first the left and then the right. Palmistry, fortune-telling, he was naturally skeptical, but he thought just for the fun of it to put his rudimentary knowledge of the art to the test. His left hand, the one indicating potential, was definitely the earth hand, indicating that the owner was practical and level-headed. On its palm he could trace the shapes and contours of the heart, head, life, and fate lines, which suggested he had a good love life, was creative, energetic, and ambitious. His right hand mirrored his left hand; the shape and contours of the heart, head, and life lines were very similar but less visible. The shape and contour of the fate line was very faint. What did it all mean? He didn't know for sure. Married for forty-five years with seven children spoke to the heart line with conviction. He was resourceful, enthusiastic, and ambitious, which mapped onto the head and life lines. Fate, that was the problem; he couldn't figure it. Were some things just meant to be, in a predetermined sequence, or did people shape their own destiny? Or did circumstances shape people?

All he knew was that he was where he was today sitting under the apple tree without knowing how he had got there. He had never set out to be anything in particular, least of all a professor. It just sort of happened to him. He looked at his hands again, turned them over, looked at knobby lumpy fingers, and smiled. His children called his hands paw's paws and his fingers Mars Bars. That was in the days before chocolate bars were downsized. Even with his lumpy old Mars Bar fingers, he could still get a tune out of the fiddle.

He bent down and picked up his old trowel in his right hand. They were still attached by some unseen umbilical. A lot of mortar had been used, bricks laid, the ghosts of scaffold glory days, but they both had made it to university. It was happenstance from mortarboard to mortarboard that was worlds apart. He wondered if he had had his palm read on leaving school could his life's journey have been foretold.

Smiling, he thought not.

Homecoming

The preparations are finished, all done, everything readied. It is that moment when waiting, the poor companion fidgets impatiently. I leave the cottage and aimlessly wander the haggard where once I helped build ricks of winter fodder for the half dozen milking cows. Beyond, my wanderings lead me among the apple trees my grandfather planted in the kitchen garden and on to the well from which I drew cold water daily. My hand, irresistibly drawn to the cast iron pump handle, forces the mechanism clanking and groaning into life, and miraculously water again flows. I look back at the cottage; it still has a cottage look about it, but now the water supply is piped in, the oil lamp light has long given way to electrification, and various efforts at home improvement have made the cottage comfortably habitable. A large inglenook fireplace dominates the family room.

It is late afternoon; daylight is fading, birds are roosting, and the air temperature is dropping, so it is getting noticeably colder. Through the window I can see the warm glow of the peat fire burning brightly. How welcoming and inviting it looks. The crisp night air carries the drifting aroma of burning peat; its earthy fragrance scents the garden, a gentle reminder of times long gone. Her shadow darkens the window, fussing over last-minute preparations. Behind me, the Maidens lighthouse's proud pillars of stone, bedrocked on the volcanic Hulin Rocks peppered around with skerries, guide seafarers safely through the North Channel. Daylight has almost gone; the beam of lighthouse light sweeps the coal black sea casting a shimmering light over the incoming tide; the plaintive call of the curlew homeward bound, a familiar childhood sound now seldom heard. I strain in the blackness of the night to see the mail boat from Stranraer, but it is too early, I know they will not have sailed yet, but still I expectantly look.

Before me Agnew's Hill cresting the ring of Sallagh barely visible, lonesome houselights spread an amber glow here and there. The people who live there watch over sheep; they live quietly among themselves. They would be lost in today's talk back, phone in radio culture; they have better things to do.

I am at the front gate now, looking south along the road from Drains Bay as it snakes its way past me out of town up through East Antrim to Belfast and far beyond. I glance back at the cottage; I am not alone. The ancestors are here; they swirl around, phantoms of the night from the town lands of Ballysnod, Killyglen, Carncastle, and Waterloo Bay's Jurassic Park's ten million years of history. I can hear the swell of the sea on Waterloo Bay's gravel beach and see the glimmer of the sea under the Maidens sweeping beam. The sea sounds are winter sounds. This night could be any night, but it is not; it is the eve of Christmas Night. They are homeward bound by air, land, and sea. Inside all is readied that could be readied. Now is the waiting time. It passes slowly.

I pace back and forth the well-trodden path to the gate, waiting, watching for approaching signals from the east and south, until they arrive at the gate, home again. I strain again against the blackness of the night searching for the mail boat from the east, plowing watery furrows toward me, so that soon I know they will be home.

I am reminded of a lad of Christmas past, homeward bound out of York Street station on the final leg of the long journey home. Crowded into second- and third-class carriages, passengers waited impatiently, listening to the hissing of the steam engine readying itself for the long haul northward, pausing at every hole in the hedge on its laborious way, and emptying itself bit by bit. The rhythmic clackety clacking of wheels on rails beating out the music of homecoming. Listening, I could imagine my mother preparing the midnight feast complete with slabs of chocolate cake stacked on the Royal Albert cake stand she kept for special occasions. I see my father too impatiently pacing the long acre.

Suddenly they are home. Molly rushes out to join me at the gate. We see their faces; tears of welcome fill our eyes; we embrace. In joyous thanksgiving we breathed an ancient prayer:

> Deep peace of a running wave to you.
> Deep peace of the flowing air to you.
> Deep peace of the quiet earth to you.
> Deep peace of the shining stars to you.
> Deep peace of the gentle night to you.
> Moon and stars pour their healing light on you.
> Deep peace to you.

They ease past us, our children, grandchildren, and the dogs, home safe. We follow them in, closing the door and shutting out the cold dark night. They find their sleeping places, dump their stuff, and gather around the wood-burning fire chattering. From the other room, through the gap between door and its frame I observe. They are happy to be home. I am glad they are here. The aging year is quietly surrendering to the birth of a new year. The moon moved through its phases is full. Now we are back from midnight mass. In former times midnight meant midnight; now midnight means 9:00 p.m. in old money; I don't hear anyone complaining.

I am standing with my back to my mother's Christmas rose and my father's handmade Christmas crib looking at the old battered record player in the corner, a 78 rpm record in hand primed to load. The room is readied for this special evening. The fire brightly burns its welcome; crisp white cloth covers the table. Candles in their once-a-year-used silver sticks pose proudly, wicks eagerly waiting for the caress of a welcome match. I look out the window into the night. The full moon silhouettes the naked trees wrapping the garden in a blue half light. I have left the room door half closed letting the sounds of family filter in.

It is time; the 78 is loaded.

At midnight exactly the needle scratches the surface of the spinning disc, releasing the opening bars of music to filter through the house. They'll say he's at it again, but they'll quieten and listen.

Then Caruso sings Placide Cappeau's "Cantique de Noel" and I duet.

> O Holy Night! The stars are brightly shining,
> It is the night of the dear Saviour's birth.
> Long lay the world in sin and error pining.
> Till he appeared and the spirit felt its worth.
> A thrill of hope the weary world rejoices,
> For yonder breaks a new and glorious morn.
> Fall on your knees! Oh, hear the angel voices!
> Oh night divine, the night when Christ was born;
> O night divine, O night O night divine!

They filter in chorusing.

Across the seas they have sailed and through the skies they have flown to gather and share the gift of family.

The carol ends, the record player resets and falls silent, and the mood is set. The room lights are dimed. My shaking hand invites a match to persuade the dormant candles into life. Mixed colors of red, green, and azure blue bathe the room in a soft hue. I look around. We are on solid ground tonight.

Slowly settled at table, Eve of Christmas supper is underway without fuss. All who could be here are here, and those not able to be here are here too, one way or another. Supper-ending small talk continuing, I ease back from the table to scan the room from the cover of candle-cast colored shadow. All is calm, all is bright; we are at peace this holy night.

It is time for our Christmas ritual of gift giving. The mound of gift-wrapped assortments under the Christmas tree is expertly excavated and distributed by eager hands. The room fills with anticipation as gifts one by one in turn are opened and revealed. Older grandchildren enrich the process, while the little believers sleep fast in blissful expectation. It is that unique interlude when no one is ever disappointed or dares reveal disappointment.

I am alone now in the quiet room. The bare table rests its weary legs waiting for the morrow's feast. The colorful wrapping paper gathered up out of sight has served its annual purpose. I stand in the half light before dawn staring through the naked window at the shadowy outline of the garden shed. Something moves. The twiggy ends of tree branches in a gentle breeze make water music on the corrugated tin shed roof. December fruit glints on the old apple tree, and frost-coated grass glitters in the frosty dawn.

Across the land families are celebrating the birth of Jesus Christ. An island people proud of its saints and scholars, once conservative, steadfast, sure of itself and its Christen trajectory today is in part liberal, irresolute, and divergent on many things including faith and morals.

Southward citizens rescinded the Eighth Amendment to their Constitution, removing equal rights for the mother and unborn child. In October past, blasphemy as an offense was also removed from their constitution. There is more to come on a woman's rights within the home.

Why not!

Here by way of contrast is the only part of the United Kingdom where abortion is illegal in almost every conceivable circumstance, with Presbyterians resolute.

I gaze with incredulity at the dawning of Christmas Day and wonder if the Presbyterians now are latter-day Catholics. The nativity morning brightens my eyes and clams my turbulent thoughts. In trust and faithfulness Mary and Joseph believed what they understood God wanted from them. But that was two millennia ago. Evolution takes many shapes and forms; it takes time, sometimes a long time. But when circumstances dictate, much can change in a generation.

I watch the winter sun in its eternal struggle to rise toward the heavens my mind conflicted. Will this island home be enriched in years to come? If I could tell you, I would let you know.

All this when a child is born?

Hope Restored

Hope woke from a fitful sleep, troubled by a recurring dream he couldn't understand. In the dream he always arrived late, too late, offered too little, wasn't needed or wanted. His inability to make sense of the dream irritated him. At breakfast with his two cousins, Faith and Charity, he felt miserable, avoided conversation, and morosely picked at his food. After a short while as the awkwardness between them stretched, he excused himself, left them at the table and went for a walk in the forest in search of a clear head. They watched him go, concerned; they knew something was troubling him; maybe they thought, *He's just overwrought.*

Meandering through the cool, dappled sunlit forest blind to all around him, Hope mulled over his dream. Inwardly he conceded that no matter how hard and earnestly he worked, everywhere in the world he went, injustice, corruption, slavery, selfishness, materialism, drug addiction—every conceivable abomination—was increasing. Evil was winning; the poor were getting poorer while the rich were getting richer. This was not how it was meant to be; he was supposed to be making a difference. He had worked tirelessly to foster in humanity an aspirational desire for a way of living embracing goodness, kindness, gentleness, steadfastness, and faithfulness. From the beginning he had set about his mission with relish twenty-four-seven, nonstop. Always on the go, couldn't sit still for a moment, too much to do. Eons passed without any tangible reduction in his workload; in fact, it was increasing. Slowly but surely a feeling that the forces working against him were becoming stronger enveloped him.

It was unsettling. Always it seemed he came up short. He was by his own judgment failing lamentably. Wandering in his forest of dark feelings he felt miserable, ineffective, and insecure. Irritation and annoyance ate at him like a swarm of hungry bloodsucking mosquitoes. He was bordering on despair.

As time passed, his wandering took him to a clearing in the forest bathed in the noonday sun. In the center of the clearing he glanced up at the sun and instinctively raised his arms to the high heavens. The heat from the huge ball of burning gas in the sky that sustained life on earth warmed him through, slowly changing the landscape of his disposition and reviving his spirit.

As the fog in his head slowly cleared, he began to understand that being humanity's caretaker was a very tough, demanding job. The emotional relief he experienced each time he answered its call had become an obsession, a craving, an addiction. Caring, healing, without him realizing it, had become the nectar to dull his feeling of inadequacy; the thought of failure was overwhelming. It was a feeling that would only subside temporarily with another supreme act of self-sacrifice. As he traversed the world slowly in his mind, he began to see as if for the first time the wonder of it, the miracle of life happening before his eyes. It dawned on him that he had lost his sense of purpose; his negative feelings were coming from a loss of perspective. It wasn't about him or his needs; it was all about suffering humanity. He was their clean bandage, a healing poultice. He needed to get a grip on himself and find his mojo.

Mentally exhausted, he sat down to rest. When he woke up he found himself lying under a blackthorn tree in the middle of a field that gently sloped down to the seashore below. When he turned his head and looked up he saw a strange-looking little fellow staring down at him. The little fellow was a leprechaun and by nature was an exceedingly engaging conversationalist. Hope realized he was in Ireland, of all places, but had no idea how he had gotten there. Aided with incisive prompting from the leprechaun, the door to Hope's heart eased open, and his soul poured out its river of worthlessness feelings. His inner hidden self was let out, and in truth he felt the better for it. The little fellow said nothing for a while as they sat looking down on the millpond sea gently lapping the shores, listening to the music of water on shingle. Then he bent down and picked a little three-leafed plant from the ground where they were sitting and started to talk. Holding up the little plant he pointed to the three leaves explaining that the number three was sacred in Celtic culture. Deities were portrayed in threes, he said: fire, breath, and water; earth, sky, and sea; father, son, and spirit. The Dagda, the Celtic father-god of the earth and ruler over life and death, the leprechaun explained, had three daughters, each one with a particular skill, and the three together worked as a team in service to their father. Each leaf on the plant, the leprechaun continued, absorbed light from the sun, transforming it into food for the plant, which was fed down through its single stem to the roots below ground, enabling it to propagate and spread with the passing of time. You and your cousins are the leaves on the stem that sustains you, and, like the daughters of Dagda, each one of you has a particular attribute that in combination is a metaphor for a particular way of life: trust, conviction, and belief. Your everlasting burden is that all humanity depends on you, now and always, for without you there is only misery and despair. You are humanity's necessity—your "Source's" gift—but you cannot shoulder humanity's burden alone. It is impossible. You must leave something for Faith and Charity to do. They sat together in silence for what seemed a long time. Breaking the silence, the little man offered Hope his help. Pointing to what looked like a black mooring buoy bobbing in gentle frequency with the calm sea, he told Hope it was an oceangoing curragh that the fisher folk had used around the coast for generations and that stretching out before them was the ocean of humanity. To help Hope find his way he would give him a choice—the curragh or a compass—with one condition to be revealed when Hope made his choice. Hope after due deliberation chose the curragh.

Stroking his long white beard and drawing himself up to his full height of thirty-five and a half inches, the leprechaun delivered his condition. Hope would no longer carry his burden alone; it would be shared with his cousins Faith and Charity. As they trawled the ocean of humanity together, Faith would be the helmsman setting the course they would follow; Charity would be the paddle powerhouse driving them forward, and Hope would be humanity's assault force combating evil with good. It was his job to ensure that evil did not have the last word. As the leprechaun continued talking he had no conception of the passage of time; only the soft lilting Irish brogue reverberated through his conciseness.

Inwardly invigorated, clear in his head—he felt he had been raised from the dead—Hope made for the curragh. He walked with a lilt, a spring in his step and joy in his heart. When he turned to wave farewell to the leprechaun, there was just a blackthorn tree in the middle of the field. Then he woke up in the clearing in the forest confused. Was it just another dream, a vision perhaps? It didn't matter because the fog in his head had lifted; he knew his role in the scheme of things. For the first time in a long time he felt unencumbered, free of expectations and fear of failure

He hurried back to greet his cousins; light was fading in the forest; it was late in the afternoon. They saw him coming and rushed out to meet him, relief and joy visible on their faces. Hope ran arms outstretched to embrace them and the future. They sat for hours as his troubled mind spoke, telling them about the conditions of people in the world waiting to be bought and sold every day. He spoke passionately about the destinies of nameless people who were nothing without them—Faith, Hope, and Charity.

Together they rejoiced and prepared to again trawl the oceans of humanity.

Love's Mantle

Departures! How many times had they followed that directional signage in bus stations, train stations, and airport terminals en route to their destination?

Today they were going to visit another place associated with departures, not from choice but out of respect for a friend who had passed, as they say—about someone who had died. The well-traversed route to the local burial ground was signposted for visitors, but for those in residence the way out was a matter of faith.

Now seniors, it seemed that the frequency of their attendance at funerals had significantly increased with the passage of time; they were trying to avoid attending as many as they possibly could. It was becoming increasingly debilitating. On this particular occasion, the passing of a dear old friend, they could not default.

It was a beautiful sunny afternoon as they made their way, suitably attired, to the funeral service, prior to the removal of the remains for interment. Funerals, like weddings, always attracted keen observers; it was always better to make the effort to look one's best. The remains—an intriguing expression often used to describe a lifeless body—leftover after the process of living has exhausted its usefulness, is a much less disrespectful term than leftovers and much easier for eulogists to mouth.

On the way to the church he remarked on the fine weather, to which his wife responded not from any depth of faith but unthinkingly, "Well, at least he's got a good day for it," which of course all depends on one's perspective on such matters. A frequently used colloquial, it reminded him of the two Irishmen lost in the middle of a desert under the blazing noonday sun. One asked the other, "What day is it?" His companion replied, "It's Saint Patrick's Day" eventually through parched cracked lips. The first fellow said, "Well, at least we got a good day for it." It turned out for them to be a very good Saint Patrick's Day, as they survived to tell the tale. The luck of the Irish! Maybe there's something in it after all.

At the requiem, the preacher in her homily used *door* as a metaphor for the threshold to be crossed when life on earth has ended, several times to explain to believers and nonbelievers alike the cliff edge transitional event that death actually is and the reward for the believer that beckons beyond. As she developed her theme, the expression "Brexit means Brexit" that politicians were repeating ad nauseam crossed his mind, together with the notion of a transitional period to ease their parting. *Purgatory*, he thought, *is the transitional holding place after death, for nearly all the less than perfect dearly departed, though the duration of any individual's transition is as clear as that pertaining to Brexit.*

Eventually, to his relief, the service ended; the small cortege formed and set off in convoy to the local cemetery. In their car following the hearse, it occurred to him that there must be a direct correlation between the age of the deceased and the number of mourners. He reckoned, using the concept of diminishing returns, that there must be some cutoff point where, as the age of the deceased increased the number of mourners decreased, leaving only a handful of genuine mourners and optimistic beneficiaries

The local cemetery occupied a desolate hillock, unfit for any profitable agricultural use. Even on a sunny day it was a desolate, cold, unwelcoming place. Having been there before many times, and primed with local knowledge, they donned their warm coats and stashed in their car on this occasion the unneeded umbrellas. Others less well prepared for the location suffered for it. The assembled mourners gathered around the open grave and stared into the gaping trench, which was a short while ago eloquently described as the door through which all must pass. He wondered if they really got it. Did the penny drop, or was it just parked conveniently away, too difficult to face. This was the threshold everyone would have to cross one day for sure one way and another; there was no get out clause.

The final committal proceedings droned on so long that his mind wandered to the day he was standing in this cemetery beside his mother at her son in-law's interment. His mother after his passing often referred to him as a "harmless cratur," meaning creature, adding to soften the putdown, "but he was always good to her," meaning her daughter. He was standing beside his mother that day, as he was standing now looking into the mouth of an empty grave, readied to be filled with the boxed-up remains when his ninety-four-year-old mother said, "This is a quare cowl spot; it would founder ye up here." He just nodded in response; she carried on rather loudly, as she was hard of the hearing, "Ouch ah wish they would hurry up and put him in the ground 'til we get outa here." He often wondered what she really thought at her age; she was only ninety-five at the time, standing looking into someone else's open grave waiting to be inhabited. He would never know; she passed less than a year after her son-in-law, joining her husband in the family plot. He would have to empty that well for himself.

Another occasion in another cemetery a long way from where he was now in time, distance, and culture came to mind. That's what going to cemeteries did to him now, brought things to mind. As if transported through time, he was standing in the graveyard in his mother's home village. Strange how just standing looking into an open grave can evoke feelings and memories long thought dormant. *Not the sort of thing you'd want to be doing too often,* he thought. The occasion was his maternal grandmother's funeral. The day before his grandmother's burial, his mother wanted to go, for reasons best known to her, to visit the grave—the family plot, as country folk often say. He was assigned the task, which he dutifully fulfilled, but unbeknown to him the gravediggers, in excavating the plot, had broken through the last coffin deposited there some considerable time ago. They had excavated through the rotted coffin and disturbed the remains of the last person interred there. In the course of their labors they had placed a skull and some large bones on the grass by the graveside. They were on their lunch break when he approached the grave a few paces ahead of his mother. He reckoned the skull was her father's, his grandfather who had been killed in an accident before he was born. If it was him, it was the first time he had set eyes on his grandfather, who he thought, if truth was told, wasn't looking his best. He wasn't daunted in any way by his discovery, but he thought his mother might be upset and sought to shield her. He needn't have bothered; she looked at the skull and bones and muttered to him, "That's me da," and without another word turned and walked away.

On reflection he shouldn't have been concerned about his mother's feelings; she was from farming stock and was used to things passing in their time, as they say. Wringing a chicken's neck never fazed her; he witnessed her doing it many times with her bare hands in the yard at home. The same hands that had shaped him one way and another. Happy days! The notion of family plot returned and furrowed his brow: a grave, a small piece of ground. Thinking about it, for country folk there might be little difference between burying and planting; recalling his nonagenarian mother's remark, "Hurry up and put him in the ground" at her son-in-law's interment. Mind you it was very cold that particular day.

His thread of thought was severed as the prayers ended. Their old friend was laid to rest; handshakes and goodbyes were exchanged, and they took their leave, duty done.

As late afternoon embraced early evening, they sat together out on the south-facing decking behind their cottage having tea. It was always their last meal of the day, and they made the most of it. He didn't know exactly when the custom started and took root; it didn't matter; it was what they did; it was them being themselves.

Facing west, he watched the luminous sun arc across a clear blue sky, toward the distant low hills behind which it would disappear from sight, the departing day making way for the arrival of night. In the great scheme of the universe, night in turn would depart from this little segment of the world, heralding the dawning of another welcome day. *Life*, he thought, *is packed full of departures and arrivals.* He was experiencing one now, as he sat still while the spinning earth orbited the sun, causing its illusory setting. Much traveled, they had eagerly waited for and witnessed glorious sunrises and sunsets in every continent. Each journey to a new destination started with a departure, but always the most welcoming thing on the journey home was the arrivals sign in the bus terminal, railway station, or airport terminal.

His thoughts as the sun set turned to their dear friend who had just passed through life's final threshold on a one-way ticket and wondered what and where his destination was and if he had been welcomed with an arrivals sign. He thought about his ninety-five-year-old mother at the graveside for her son-in-law's interment and her remark and wondered, *As we get older, do we just accept the fact that we are mortal?* When young, such thoughts never enter your mind; youthfulness blends into maturity, and living carries on. Shakespeare described it as the seven ages of man, he remembered from his schooling. He thought of it, the seven phases of man, each preceding phase fertilizing and growing the succeeding phase before being jettisoned. As he pondered, he substituted forms for phases. *In the process of living,* he thought, *we morph—take different forms at different times—the termination of each form in the scheme of things a minideath without grief. It is only at the final threshold that grief enters as the unwelcome guest, conception the first form of being an unseen metamorphose. Could it be*, he thought, *that death is the same?* When his turn came, would he metamorphose? The nagging thought was what form would he assume?

It was getting cooler; the sun had gone, and night had silently wrapped them up. It was time to put his thoughts to rest; tomorrow was another day full of surprises. Yesterday's self, he knew, was the seed for tomorrow's plant. He didn't kneel by his bedside to say his night prayers, as he did as a child, anymore. His approach to prayer now, contemplative, mined different levels within the deep recesses of his mind. As they lay in bed together inviting sleep in the meadowland of shared delight, he thought about the threshold that one of them would cross without the other, the parting of their ways. It was an unwelcome thought.

That time would come, he knew, when the burden of life deadens their willing shoulders. Silently he prayed that the welcoming clay would nourish their seeding bodies into new forms, in the communion of the ancestors. Drifting to sleep he felt an invisible cloak of love softly surrond them in its gentle embrace.

One Saturday Morning

The alarm clock on the bedside table noisily came to life at five thirty on a summer Saturday morning. He stretched out a hand to silence it before it would rouse his wife, Mary. The sun was already up, encouraging blackbirds into song. He played golf every Saturday morning in a four ball with pals he had gone to school with and always looked forward with relish to these weekend encounters.

Paddy Frame was in his sixty-sixth year, recently retired from a career in teaching. Yawning and stretching, he moved noiselessly on the bedroom floor to where he had laid out his golfing gear, the night before—socks, pants, matching shirt, and jumper—and stealthily tiptoed to the bedroom door. Satisfied that he had not disturbed Mary, he exited the bedroom, closing the door quietly behind him. Downstairs he showered, shaved, and made himself ready for tee off. Everything he needed was set out the night before—golf clubs, trolley, and shoes awaited him in his car—all he had to do was load in the trolley battery and a change of clothes and head off. He breakfasted on fruit juice and cereal. He would have preferred coffee, but boiling the kettle was too noisy, too big a risk of disturbing Mary's sleep, so he chose to do without. As he ate his cereal he glanced occasionally at the kitchen clock; their allotted tee off time was six thirty, and he wanted to be there with plenty of time in hand. It was their preferred time, their morning, their gathering. With a final glance at the clock, he rose, pocketed a couple of bananas, and slipped quietly out the back door locking it behind him. In the garden shed; he unplugged the trolley battery, closed the shed doors, opened the garage door, unlocked his car, put the battery into the boot and the bananas into his golf bag, hung up his change of clothes in the back of the car, reversed out onto the street, electronically closing the garage door behind him, and set off.

Paddy was feeling good, looking forward to meeting up with his pals and enjoying the friendly banter. Seat belt fastened, he was on his way, the morning sun already high in the cloudless sky to his right. Although it was summer, it was too early in the morning for the usual stream of tour buses to be winding their way along the coast road. He had the road to himself. It was not far from his house to Cairnmount Golf Club. He had been a member there for over fifty years but had long given up playing competitive golf. His handicap, now eight, had once been as low as three, but he was content with eight at his age. Now he enjoyed a so-called friendly four ball with his pals. He could relax and enjoy the freedom of the course—the scale of it, the wildlife, and most of all the feeling of being part of a much bigger inclusive landscape. He loved this short drive to the golf club; it was only five or six miles, no distance. But on a beautiful summer's morning like this morning with the rising sun coloring the tranquil turquoise sea and the prospect of glimpsing the western isles of Scotland, Paddy was as happy as a child splashing in a muddy puddle. He drove along enjoying the freedom of the deserted road carefully keeping within the forty-mile-an-hour speed limit, in his element, his time, and his beautiful morning.

Savoring the peace and tranquility of the early morning, his attention was drawn to a lonesome elevated bungalow, set well back from the road on his left, which used to belong to the Weston family. Once upon a time he had been friends with the daughter of the house, Beth, but that was a long time ago. He didn't know who lived there now. Something that looked like yellowish shimmers of sunlight on the big picture window at the front of the bungalow caught his eye. He remembered being in that very room and the magnificent views from it out over the sea toward the Mull of Kintyre, the western isles, and beyond. The morning sunlight danced like fire on the window glass, flickering and shimmering, iridescent illumination. A little further on down the road, something caused him to think about what he had just experienced, seen. What exactly was it? The sun's rays on the window reflected as shimmery light in hues of primrose, dirty yellow, blues and greens—or yellow luminous flickering flames?—behind the window in the house. Was it his imagination? He tried to focus on his golf game, but a house on fire! Could this be for real? Had he just ignored it? Was he so single-minded, destination orientated, that he had just driven on past? What if someone was in the house?

Suddenly without another thought he stood on the brakes, slewing the car across the road to a halt. Fortunately for him and any other hapless road user, there was no oncoming traffic. He did the quickest three-point turn he had ever done in his life and hared back up the road as fast as he could go. Reaching the house, he stopped and jumped out of the car. His worst fears were confirmed; he could see the yellow flames licking the window glass. The house was on fire, well on fire.

When he went to play golf he always took his mobile phone; it was a habit started after he witnessed a golfer collapsing on the sixteenth green many years ago. Mobile phones and buggies were a new thing then, a novelty. It had taken a long time for someone to run all the way back to the clubhouse and telephone for help and for an ambulance to arrive at the sixteenth green. In the end, it was too late. Today there was a defibrillator in the clubhouse. He knew a guy who carried one in his buggy. Prepared as he thought he was for an emergency on the golf course, he hadn't seen this one coming. He dialed 999, asked for the fire service, told them that the house was on fire, and gave the location and whatever information he could.

Standing on the road, not only could he see the flames; he could hear window glass cracking. Soon it would shatter and collapse; the room would be totally engulfed—an inferno—and the fire would spread inside and outside the bungalow. *What if there is someone in the house?* he asked himself. Throwing caution to the wind, he bolted up the flights of stone steps that led to the front door of the bungalow. It was a solid timber door. He tried opening it, but it was locked. There was no way he could force an entry. He could hear the double-glazed window glass stressing and cracking under the assault of the intense heat of the fire. He could feel the heat too, partially shielded from it as he was.

Paddy ran around the side of the house past the oil tank searching for the back door. It was a four-glazed panel door giving access to the interior of the dwelling through the kitchen. It was locked too. He could see the back door key in the lock on the inside; there was smoke in the kitchen, not a lot yet, but it was slowly filling up. He frantically looked around for something to break the glass, but he couldn't find anything. In desperation, risking injury, he braced himself and tried to put his foot through the bottom pane of glass.

The double-glazed panel cracked but didn't break; he kicked it again, making a hole big enough to get a hand through. He reached in and up and unlocked the door. Then he discovered the door was bolted top and bottom. He undid the bottom bolt and then scoured the area at the rear of the house again desperately looking for something, anything, to break the top pane of glass; he couldn't find anything, and precious time was being wasted. In desperation he ran back to the door and kicked in the jagged pieces of glass still hanging in the door frame at the bottom of the door until the gap was big enough to crawl through. Inside the kitchen he undid the top bolt, and the door swung open. *What now?* he thought as blood trickled from a gash on his hand.

There was some smoke in the kitchen; the kitchen door was slightly ajar, and so he closed it to keep the smoke out of the kitchen while he figured out what to do. He knew from watching television and films that smoke was the real danger in domestic fires. Victims were usually quickly overcome by smoke inhalation before the fire ever reached them. He knew that the best thing to do was to keep out of it and to get away from it, but if there were people in the house, he knew he had to do something; he just couldn't stand by and watch!

He had come this far—too late to turn back now. In the kitchen he found some towels, soaked them in water, and draped them around his head, neck, and shoulders. Tentatively he opened the kitchen door to the corridor that connected to the other rooms. There was smoke in the corridor at the ceiling, slowly building down. He had a choice: close the kitchen door behind him to keep the smoke in the corridor or leave it open. Open it would let smoke escape from the corridor, giving more time to look for occupants; at worst it would let more air in to fuel the fire. When the big picture window in the fire room eventually blew out, it wouldn't matter anyway. He left the kitchen door open.

The smoke was now quickly building down close to his head; he could feel the heat. His hair was singeing; he could smell it, taste it. He had to crouch down to keep below the smoke layer. It was seeping out from gaps around the door of the fire room. He reached up for the door handle, touched it, and quickly pulled his hand away. It was very hot. He knew that if anyone was in that room they were most certainly dead, and if he opened the door he would probably end up dead as well as anybody else in the house. He didn't open it.

Anxiously crouching down under the hot, oppressive smoke layer, he tried to remember the layout of the bungalow. Down the corridor on his right there was a room at the back of the house. Crouching lower, almost on all fours, he ran his hand along the skirting board searching for the door to that room and found it. The door handle was cool to his touch; he opened the door and crawled in. It was a bedroom, hazy with smoke but nothing like the smoke in the corridor, which was now spilling into the room through the door he had opened. Someone was lying on top of the bed asleep, a woman; he shook her, but she only moaned in response. Then he saw an empty wine bottle, wineglass, and box of pills on the bedside table. She was lying on top of a duvet; he pulled it and the woman on it onto the floor and started to drag her out of the room toward the smoke-logged corridor to safety.

The smoke layer was much lower than before; it was hotter too and was almost overwhelming. He fell to his knees and crablike dragged the duvet with the woman on it along the corridor out through the kitchen into the fresh air. Paddy was knackered. Lying on the paved area outside the house trying to get his breath back, he was stunned when the woman stirred and muttered, "Where's my daughter?"

He knew conditions inside the house were rapidly deteriorating; he also knew he had to do something. He had to try and save her daughter. It was at this moment of mental turmoil that he wondered if he had remembered to take his blood pressure tablets before he left home. It was an intrusive, distracting thought that strangely cleared his mind. He stooped below the black smoke pouring out through the open back door, reentered the kitchen, soaked towels in water again, and wrapped them around his head, neck, and shoulders. Then he soaked a tea towel in water too, wrapped it around his mouth and nose, and crawled back into the corridor, which was now pitch black. The other bedroom was at the front of the house almost opposite the one he had dragged the woman out of. The smoke layer was now only about half a meter above the floor; he crawled down the corridor slowly on all fours with his eyes half-closed. His mouth and nose were touching the floor boards.

As he crawled along, he could occasionally feel jets of fresh air sucked in by the greedy fire coming up in through the floor boards; in this predicament they were like oases in a desert—sources of fresh air, a lifeline. He needed to mark them, if he was to have any chance of getting back out alive. As good fortune would have it, today was his day for golf, and in preparation he had pocketed a handful of golf tees before leaving home, the big ones. Each time he discovered an air inlet he stuck a couple of golf tees in between the floor boards to mark it. *Pity they are not luminescent like the strips of stuff they put on the floors,* he thought, but they were all he had—a lifesaver, maybe. Crawling doggedly on, he found the bedroom door for which he was searching.

The door handle was cool to his touch; he opened it and crawled in. The room, hazy with smoke, was filling up fast with the door open; he closed it behind him. Looking around, he found the bed; it was empty. As the room slowly filled with smoke, he searched the bed and under the bed but found no one. As he was about to get out of the room, he spotted in the corner of the room a small wardrobe. He knew from working with children that sometimes when frightened they would hide themselves away.

He crawled to the wardrobe, opened it, and inside found a little, curled up, frightened girl. "It's all right. We are going to be safe. Come with me; your mummy's waiting outside for you, okay?" Gently he coaxed her out of the wardrobe and told her quietly exactly what he wanted her to do. "Crawl on your tummy along the corridor with me to the kitchen and out through the back door, okay?" She nodded. "Hold your breath for as long as you can. It'll be very hot, and we have to crawl as fast as we can. As we go, we will find little pegs sticking out of the floorboards like this one, okay?" He took a tee peg out of his pocket; it was a bright yellow one, and he showed it to her. "Okay?" She nodded. "That's where the fresh air is coming in; we can breathe it, so do as I do, okay?" She took hold of his hand. He unwrapped one of the wet towels from around himself and wrapped it around her head, neck, and shoulders and stretched it down her back as far as it could go. He knew their lives were on the line; it was going to be touch-and-go.

On their bellies side by side they crawled to the bedroom door and opened it. The intensely hot smoke was almost on top of them. He could taste it—bitter, choking, acrid. She gripped his hand tighter; she was frightened, and he was afraid for both of them and far from sure they would make it out alive. He was afraid burning bits of the ceiling would crash down on top of them. It was an old house built fifty-odd years ago; he had no idea how long it could resist the onslaught of a ferocious fire. They were through the bedroom door into the corridor when he heard her gasping for breath; he couldn't hold his breath much longer either. They had to keep moving and find a fresh air vent he had marked in the floor, just about a meter or so down the corridor. She was gasping, frantically making loud rasping guttural noises; her little body was uncontrollably violently shaking. He thought he had missed the tee pegs he had planted in the floor boards; a prayer flashed across his mind, when his free hand fanning out in front snagged the pegs. He dragged her head over to it and pushed her face down to the floor boards; "open your mouth and breathe," he commanded. "Breathe," he shouted, swallowing another mouthful of smoke in the process. He heard her gulping in the fresh air as he pressed his mouth to the floor boards too and sucked in the lifesaving fresh air. It tasted to him like cold mountain spring water. He was greedy for the air. So was she. He could hear her gulping it in. How long they lay there relieving their tortured lungs he didn't know, but the smoke was getting hotter; he was sure of that.

The smoke in the corridor was about as low as it could get; his shirt and trousers were singeing; he could feel it. The towels were losing their cooling wetness. They had to move. By his estimation the next fresh air floor vent was about two meters farther down the corridor, right in the middle of it. "Okay, take a deep breath, and let's go," he said, but as he moved he felt her hesitation. "We have to move," he barked. "Okay? Take a deep breath, and let's go. Move." He took a breath and grasped her tighter, prepared to drag her if she froze, but she was moving alongside him.

They found the air vent easily enough and gratefully put their mouths to the cracks in the floorboards. She was gasping and choking on the acrid smoke as it filled her nostrils, throat, and lungs; so was he. Paddy was burning; he could smell burned hair and flesh. His trousers were hot; he reached down to move them and touched the child on her leg. Her lower limbs were uncovered; they were slowly being cooked. He tore the damp towel off his head, only it wasn't so damp anymore, and stretched lengthways to cover her exposed legs. When the blast of heat from the smoke layer just above his head hit him, he thought his head was going to explode. He remembered he was wearing a jumper; he shrugged it off and pulled it over his head, gaining some momentary relief from the intense heat. They were only a couple of meters from the kitchen door; he could see light and knew there was another fresh air vent in the floor near the door. He had to do something and quick. He shouted at the child, telling her to take a deep breath and get ready to go on the count of three. They scrambled spiderlike toward the kitchen door and made it to where he had stuck some tee pegs into the floor; they breathed fresh air again. They gulped it in, lungs heaving, hearts pounding, muscles aching, minds racing. Air had never tasted so good except he wasn't tasting it; he was devouring it as a hungry bear would devour a carcass.

Across the kitchen he could see the smoke flowing out through the back door as fresh air was sucked in by the fire; it needed the oxygen to fuel its fury. As the outflowing smoke got nearer to the back door of the house, the incoming air forced it upward, making a bigger gap between the floor and the smoke layer. It was also a little cooler at floor level. Not much but enough to make a difference—a lifesaving difference. *Now or never*, he thought, and holding the child close said, "When I tell you to, take a deep breath, get on to your knees, run as low as you can as fast as you can out through the back door, I will follow you, okay?"

"Okay," she uttered.

"Ready," he grunted. "Take a deep breath and *run,*" he yelled. And she did.

When he saw she was halfway to the door, he started to run out too. The floor was wet and slippery; he slipped and banged his head on the ceramic tiled floor. He was almost there—outside—but not quite. Fortunately he was lying in the cooler clean air layer, but it was still very hot. He was gathering himself together to crawl to the door when a little face peering over the back door threshold said, "Come on; I'm waiting for you." He was still smiling when he fell out over the back door threshold onto the paving outside and gratefully gulped in the fresh air. He filled and emptied his lungs in quick succession while spitting out of his mouth the taste of fire and smoke that he had swallowed. Gathering himself, he focused on what was happening, and what he next needed to do.

Over on the grass, the woman was still sitting clearly disorientated, confused. The child was standing just a little way away from him. He could smell her. Smell her burned flesh, or was it his? Maybe both, he didn't know for sure, but the odor of burned flesh hung in the air like farm muck spread on fields in early spring. He looked at the child, and she looked back at him. The once wet towels clung to her, and then he realized they were stuck to her. They would have to be peeled away from her flesh, what was left of it. She shivered as he looked at her. He moved toward her, knelt in front of her, took her in his arms, and gently held her; then he took off his smelly jumper and put it around her shoulders to keep her warm. He was afraid she might be in shock. The fire was still burning fiercely. He could feel the heat where they were standing outside, so slowly he moved them away to the back of the garden, out of harm's way. It was as well he did.

They had only reached the back of the garden when the fire erupted through the roof, bringing it down in a shower of flaming debris. Then he heard the welcome shrill sound of a fire engine responding to his call for help. As the sound of the approaching fire engine grew louder, he looked back up the road he had traveled this morning, only minutes ago it seemed, and saw coming round the bend the reassuring blue flashing lights signaling that help had arrived. *Thank God*, he thought as he uncontrollably released all of the tension that had inhabited his entire being. The child looked curiously at him. *No wonder*, he thought; he was shaking. He smiled a smile to her. "It's okay; it's all over. We're safe now."

That's how the fire officer wearing the big white helmet found them—a dirty, smelly threesome tableau in a back garden on a fine summer's Saturday morning. It would have been funny looking—the woman in her nightwear sitting on the grass, the little girl wrapped up in long clinging towels with a man's dirty jumper around her shoulders, and him holding her close to him—if it wasn't so pitiful. The fire officer wanted to know if there was anyone else in the house. Paddy just shrugged; the fire officer wasn't pleased. *Doesn't really matter now*, Paddy thought. *Anyone else in there is dead for sure.* Just as the paramedics arrived, he felt sick. Suddenly there seemed to be people everywhere; it was too much for him. Someone asked how he felt. "Like throwing up," he muttered.

"Best thing you could do," was the reply. He got up, staggered over to the garden hedge and threw up—emptied his guts. All that came up was thick black treacle-like foul-smelling mess. He felt like a muck spreader, spewing his guts everywhere, glad to get rid of it, retching and retching until he could physically retch no more, until someone took him away, cleaned him up and gave him oxygen.

Sometime later, he didn't know how long, he was sitting on the roadside curb beside the ambulance. He was wondering how he had gotten there, when the woman and the little girl were brought down to be put into the ambulance. The child was lying on a stretcher. He got to his feet unsteadily and went over to them, looked down on the child, and as she gazed up at him, he bent over and kissed her brow and touched her hand. She smiled back up at him. He looked up at the burned-out shell of what was once their home, turned to the woman, and asked if she had any friends or family he could contact for her. She didn't speak. He asked her if they had anywhere to stay when they left the hospital. She just shook her head. Before he could stop himself he offered them shelter if they needed it, until they got themselves sorted. She looked at him in a way that he wondered if she really understood yet what had happened.

Then they were quickly loaded into the ambulance and whisked off to the hospital. As they departed the scene, he wondered if the child would need skin grafting on her legs; the backs of her legs were badly burned. She had never once cried out in pain as they belly crawled their way out of that house through the smoke and heat. *She's a tough little lady all right*, he was thinking to himself when the fire officer with the big white helmet loomed over him again, took him to the side of the fire engine, sat him down, and invited Paddy to tell his story from start to finish. When he finished the fire officer said, "I suppose that's your car over there with the door lying open, the keys in it, and the engine running, eh? You're lucky it wasn't nicked." The fire officer retreated to attend to other things when a pair of police officers, a man and a woman, approached Paddy; they just wanted contact details for their follow-up inquiries.

The paramedics checked him out thoroughly before eventually declaring him fit to go home, provided he avoided strenuous activity for a while. "How does a shower and bed sound?" Paddy asked, as he walked to his car. He was about to get into his car when he took stock of himself; he was a complete mess, and he was stinking. Mary would have a fit if he got into their new car in the state he was in. He remembered the change of clothes he had put in the car and his golfing wet gear in the trunk. No doubt about it; it would have to be the wet gear. He stood on the pavement half naked, half screened by the car; it didn't really matter, as there was no through traffic; the police had closed the road. Stripped almost naked putting on his waterproof trousers, jacket, and cap, he was a strange sight on a sunny summer's morning, and sure enough the firefighters packing up their gear, some of whom he had taught, offered some friendly helpful advice.

With an appropriate gesture to them Paddy set off for home laughing until the laughing became almost hysterical, and he had to get a grip—regain control of himself. It was only a couple of miles back up to his home, just enough time for him to pull himself together.

He parked in his driveway as usual; the neighbors wouldn't notice he was in his bare feet and wearing wet gear on a summer morning. They might notice that he was back home unusually early; neighbors notice deviations from routine. Paddy gathered up his smelly clothes and shoes from the boot of the car and stuffed them out of sight of the neighbors into a large plastic bag Mary always kept in the car for the weekly shopping. Closing the trunk, he went through the garage passing the garbage bin, paused, turned back, lifted the lid, and dumped his bag of clothes less the shoes into it and put the lid back on the bin. He kept the shoes; after all they were a good pair of Barkers, thinking he might be able to salvage them.

Quietly he entered the house as he had left it earlier by the back door. *Back doors, I've had my fill of those today*, he thought, and headed for the bathroom. He was looking forward to a very long luxurious shower. The solar water heating panel he had installed on the south-facing roof ensured that at this time of year there was always a plentiful supply of hot water, providing he got to use it before Mary turned on the washing machine. Then he chanced to look in the mirror. He could not believe what he saw. His face was scorched and smudged with black soot; his eyebrows were gone; his hair was frizzled and frazzled, and his hands were black. He was and looked a complete and utter mess.

When the water was gushing from the showerhead, he stepped

right into the middle of it. It couldn't be any hotter than what he had experienced earlier in that house fire, he thought. It wasn't. He dumped handfuls of shampoo over himself, lathering away with gusto striving to get the smell of acrid smoke off him—the taste of it out of his mouth—and the soot and smoke out of his hair, eyes, and ears. If only he could get the water to jet up his nose to rid himself of the smell and gunge. He worked at it, kept the hot water spewing from the showerhead, didn't know for how long, until he heard Mary call out to him, "You're back early today, Paddy, everything okay?"

"Sure," he answered through the bathroom door while turning off the shower "Everything's fine."

Then by the way of conversation she asked, "How did the golf go?" not that Mary had the least bit of interest in golf. She was glad of it because it got Paddy out from under her feet and out of her domain for a few hours every week. Oh yes, as far as Mary was concerned, golf was just men chasing a tiny white ball around a big long field trying to get it into a wee hole. Without thinking,

Paddy replied, "Sure, didn't I burn it up today," and as he spoke he almost choked on the words and set off a bout of coughing.

"Are you okay in there, Paddy," Mary asked through the door.

"Fine, Mary love, just fine I'll be finished in a minute."

Well it wasn't a minute; it was several long minutes. He needed to tidy himself up and gather himself together before facing Mary. When he emerged from the bathroom, having done the best he could, Mary was in the kitchen. He went in; he had to. She had her back to him preparing breakfast; as she spoke about something she turned to look at him to make some point or other and half turned back to what she was doing before she did a second take to look at him again. Her eyes opened wide, and her mouth dropped in astonishment. "Jesus, Paddy, what has happened to you?" she asked. He sat her down, told her the story from start to finish. She just shook her head in complete disbelief, but her maternal instinct took over. "You need a cup of tea," she said, rising to put the kettle on.

Maybe something stronger than tea would be better, he was thinking, but then again maybe not; they only do that in the movies.

When the tea was poured, he could see the questions forming in Mary's eyes. "Oh there's something else," he said. Her look invited him to carry on. "The police said they would call to follow up to take my statement. Give the neighbors something to think about, don't you think?" He smiled. She waited. *She knows there's something else. How do women do it? Are they cats, or do they have other senses?* "Anyway," he blurted out, "the woman and the child have nowhere to go when they leave the hospital, so I said they could stay with us for a few days until they get sorted out, if that is okay with you."

Several moments of silence followed; she was gathering herself, he knew, and then she got up from her chair and slowly turned away.

"Where are you off to?" he asked her.

Mary stopped and turned back to him folding her arms in front of her saying, "I am going to prepare the guest room," with a hint of a smile caressing her face. Just then the front door bell rang. *Who in the name of all that is holy is that?* he thought when Mary called out in a voice loud enough for all the neighbors to hear, "Paddy, it's the police for you." He went to the door to meet them, and looking out he could see their distinctive chevron-marked police car parked right in front of his house.

Across the street he thought he saw a window blind flicker in the sunlight.

Requiem

She had been ill for several years but deftly concealing any hint of it from her family, until eventually she could conceal it no longer. As her physical condition deteriorated, she was persuaded to see her doctor. She tried telling herself it was nothing to worry about, just a routine consultation. She described how she felt; her doctor inquired about the usual diagnostic indicators, including the passing of blood, irregular bowel movements, and much more. Samples of blood were taken for testing, and another consultation was arranged. In the weeks between appointments, she busied herself as best she could to dull her mind and suspend all its internal animations. Still worry nibbled at her, but she clung to hope as a drowning man would cling in desperation to a straw. Outwardly to family and friends she was normal; inwardly she was a twirling tangled mess of emotions.

She sat in the surgery waiting room for her second consultation; her mind, no longer suspended, was so full of fear and dread that it could entertain no other thoughts. Suddenly her name beckoned on the appointments monitor; it was her turn. She stood up and walked as a drunk walked when trying to act sober, just hoping her rubbery legs wouldn't fail her.

Sitting hands tightly clasped, face-to-face with her doctor, she felt like a child summoned to the head teacher's office, to answer for some misdemeanor. It was a foolish thought; she had to slam shut the doors of her senses. Before he even opened his mouth, she knew the worst; it was in his eyes. It was cancer—bowel cancer. He wasn't blunt; he was kind, gentle, matter of fact, and very professional. Feeling numb, her mind so overwhelmed by the thought of bowel cancer that it had no room for any other thought, she fought to get a grip on her emotions. The whirlpool of confused feelings within her abated sufficiently for her to understand that an urgent consultation with a cancer specialist was being arranged. Eventually it was time for her to leave the doctor to care for his other patients. Politely she thanked him, while at the same time wondering why any sane person could thank anyone for telling them they had bowel cancer. It was everything she had dreaded but could never countenance—cancer, bowel cancer.

Leaving the surgery, her heart felt like it had been ruthlessly pushed through a bacon slicer. Her way home took her past a chapel; she went in and found a secluded place and tried to gather her thoughts and find some coherence. Breathing slowly and deeply as she did when meditating, calmness gradually settled on her. In that quiet place her whole life went revolving around in the eye of her mind, like a carousel with its highs and lows and ups and downs. Eventually inwardly resigned to her condition, a coldness creeping over her forced her to leave the chapel and make her way home. Inside she dropped her house keys beside the telephone. Soon it would start ringing, and she would have to tell her children, all six of them, the "news." She dreaded it, but it could not be avoided; it had to be done. Feeling a little tired, she went into her bedroom, closed the blinds, and lay down in the darkened room. As she lay there it dawned on her that nothing much had changed yet. Life, she realized, goes on, with or without you, behind closed doors and curtained windows or wherever. It was up to her to get up and get on with it or lie down beaten into submission by a silent, insidious mutant cell. She decided what she would do, and feeling strangely good, she got up ready to embrace her family.

In the months that followed she was seen by several cancer specialists, underwent more tests, and picked up bits of information, like the difference in growth behavior in normal and cancer cells. She learned something about oncology. Her oncologist, as she called him, was a nice young man with a soft southern Irish accent, beautiful brown eyes, and an easy smile. She liked him, and she had confidence in him.

Three months on from her original diagnosis she sat in a hospital consulting room listening to her consultant giving his considered opinion on the likely progress of her cancer and the treatments that could be employed to control, if not eradicate it. It was also impressed on her that her cancer was particularly aggressive. Her mind diverted—her cancer, that phrase started to needle her, it was so personal, her possession, her thing, she didn't own it, God knows she didn't want it, it was so invasive, but in the end she conceded it was hers all right, and it wasn't going anywhere. The storm in her head passed without external expression.

So began extensive treatments: curative chemotherapy, to begin with, followed by radiotherapy with all the attending side effects—nausea, hair loss, tiredness, weakness, and irritability. It was a grueling course of treatment, but she never flagged; she stuck with it and saw it through.

After her course of treatments was completed and further scans taken, she once more sat with a consultant to learn if the treatments she had endured had proved worthwhile. It was good news; she was in remission, partial remission. Relief flooded over her like water cascading over a dam filled beyond its capacity. She felt as if the sentence of death looming over her had been miraculously lifted. Partial remission was explained to her. The tumor was still there, but it had begun to shrink. The frequency and intensity of her treatments were reduced coupled with cautious hopeful observation.

Two busy years passed quickly before little things began to suggest to her that perhaps all was not well. Further consultations followed. The cancer had returned, but in effect she realized it had never gone away. It had recuperated, got better, got stronger, and was growing. In the end she was told that surgery was the only viable option. She had a choice: do nothing or surgery. She chose surgery. Her bowel was surgically removed, a colonoscopy bag was fitted, and the five-hour-long operation was declared successful. After sufficient rest and recovery she was discharged from the hospital. In the cul-de-sac of identical semidetached town houses where she lived, there was little evidence of neighborliness. People kept themselves to themselves, just as she did. But she was beginning to notice things, to listen to words spoken, with increased sensitivity. She was ready to fight. *Damn it,* she thought, *I am not in a wheelchair yet.* With that thought in mind, she went with purpose into her small garden to vent her fury weeding.

Three years quickly passed, drifting into memory. Blissfully engaged with her family, two more grandchildren had arrived; she was unaware of the minute changes occurring in the cells in her body. As yet they were undetectable. One day playing with one of her grandchildren she suddenly felt as if her whole insides were burning. She knew immediately that it was back. It was "like waking on the best day of your life to feel this immortal living thing inside her," as Plumly in his poem "Cancer" had put it.

After further extensive consultations, examinations, and tests, she found herself once more sitting in the presence of her consultant listening to him gently telling her that he could do nothing for her. She didn't move or blink; she couldn't. She just wished she was deaf. He was talking, but she wasn't hearing anything after he had said, "I am very sorry, but there is nothing I can do for you, nothing." The word *nothing* seemed to explode from his mouth. Never before had the word *nothing* taken on such a meaning. She had just been given a death sentence.

She thought of her father, a joiner by trade. She knew what he did to rotten timber; he tore it out and burned it. All she wanted now was her father, anybody, to reach inside her and tear out the rot that was consuming her from within. He couldn't do that. Lung cancer had taken him when she was very young. It was a long time since his claw hammer had made music down the garden in his shed. A hint of a smile struggled for daylight across her tight lips, even though she knew she was rotting away inside. They had tried to poison it, burn it, cut it out, but it had survived—endured it all. It was stronger than her. It had won; it had a life of its own. The only consolation was that its winning would be short-lived; it would die with her too. She would win the end game.

She had sat quite still throughout the consultation. She knew he was observing her closely, gauging her reactions wondering if he needed to suggest counseling. *Funny,* she thought, thinking, *clearly now after all these meetings and everything we've been through together, he and the others don't really know neither me, nor I them. Better that way;* she thought. *We all can get on with our lives whatever that means, or as far as I am concerned what little's left of it. Will he tell me before I leave,* she thought, *how long I have got left, or should I ask him?* Eventually she did ask. "Difficult to say, months maybe," he answered. They sat in silence looking at nothing, for a long time, not engaging, until she realized there was nothing more to say.

Politely they disengaged. He went back to his work, his vocation, something he was called to do and did every day with immense kindness and consideration. Why else would anyone do it? Then she prepared herself for home. It was then that it struck her forcefully that he must do this every day, tell people they had no future. How awful for him. Making her way out through the hospital entrance foyer, she felt anonymous, invisible, insignificant, a nothing, a nobody. Reaching the busy thoroughfare outside, she stood somewhat bewildered on the pavement observing the nonstop flow of traffic. Slowly a calmness settled on her, and for the first time she realized that people received the diagnosis she had just received every day. The only difference was that today was her day; it was her turn. The taxi ride up from the city center bus station to the hospital had taken no time at all, so she decided to walk back. She had plenty of time, smiling to herself at the thought that time had for her acquired a whole new nuance, to catch the next bus back home.

As she walked her mind galloped over her life, caressing moments of particular joy. She was sixty-six just past. Her husband Roy had passed away before his time twenty years ago.

When her husband died she ran the family business and raised their family all by herself. Yes she was a doer all right. She saw them through university, married, and well settled before she relinquished the business. Owning and managing a green grocer's in the town single-handed and raising a family at the same time was no easy task, but she persevered.

It was the early winter's mornings driving up to the markets that finally persuaded her to give it up when she did.

With all sorts of thoughts coursing through her mind she found herself at the city center bus station hardly knowing how she got there. Waiting for her bus, she pulled the collar of her coat up around her face, hoping that she wouldn't meet anyone she knew. Not that they would know one way or the other the outcome of her consultation. No, it was just that she was unsure of herself, how she might respond to some innocuous chance remark. Tension was building inside her, and she knew it. All she wanted to do was to get home, lock the door, and keep the world at bay until she could come to terms with her predicament. "Predicament, some bloody predicament, you idiot; wise up, get a grip," she muttered as she talked to herself.

Her bus was on time. She boarded without encountering anyone she knew and was glad of that. Taking her seat at the rear of the coach, she hunkered down pretending to be asleep. It was raining heavily. They cleared the congested city and found the open road. She didn't know if it was the motion of the bus and metronomic swishing of the windscreen wipers that caused it, but she found herself thinking of her parents—her mother petite and particular, her father coarse and common. Yet somehow they managed to sidestep and tiptoe through the minefield of their cultural differences, producing nine children in the process. She was piggy in the middle with four brothers and four sisters. She liked symmetry. All her siblings were alive and well, but they were not what might be described as a close family. They loved each other but not demonstrably. With a big family there had to be order, routine, and a place for everything and everything in its place. She remembered they had separate drawers for their clothes and personal things in the bedroom the girls shared; a place for everything and everything in its place including feelings and emotions. Order and routine shaped the person she was to become. Lost in her musings, the bus arrived at her stop. Thankfully it had stopped raining; she would make it home dry.

Sitting in her living room in her armchair with an espresso in hand, she looked around taking it all in. In interior designer's jargon it was minimalistic, clean hard surfaces, no clutter, and a place for everything and everything in its place. Every room in her home was the same: devoid of personality, her hidden self formed in childhood from obedience to order and routine. But appearances could be deceiving; inwardly she felt like an animal that in its maturing and seasoning had shed its outer wrapper. She had worked hard at overcoming parental influences that curtailed expression of feelings, and she knew that as far as her own family was concerned she had succeeded. Perhaps she had added other spices for flavor. Time would tell, but she wasn't going to be around to savor it.

Finished with her coffee, notebook and pen in hand, she set about compiling a list of must-do things. Mother's Day was just over a week away. This year it fell on a Sunday. That's when she decided she would give her family the news, when they were all together here with her, as they were every year, in her home for dinner on Mother's Day. It was her favorite day of the year. She would tell them the funeral directors she had chosen, instructed and paid, the order of service for her requiem Mass, and the contents of her will, among other bits and pieces she wanted done before her final curtain call.

As the weeks stretched, she could feel the thing inside her growing, getting stronger, and demanding more from her. Her family coped as best they could; home care packages were put in place in addition to occasional inpatient hospice care.

On the June Monday morning she left her home in the ambulance for the hospice, the sun was brightly shining; she knew she would not be coming back. She was saying goodbye to cul-de-sac semidetached neighborliness forever, and in a strange way she was glad to be out of it.

In the hospice she shared a ward with five other people, cautiously getting to know them, sharing and talking. Although every day was always only twenty-fours, in the hospice it seemed much longer. Her children heeded her advice and organized a visiting schedule so that the burden, as she saw it, of visiting was shared. She knew that weekends would bring the gatherings. Her brothers and sisters visited then when they could fit it in, but when her final curtain call would come, they would gather en masse.

When she was moved from the shared ward into a private room, she knew her time was ebbing fast. She would fight to the end, but the living and immortal thing inside her would triumph. She accepted that in the knowledge that she would have the last laugh. Content in mind, she prepared for the gathering of family before medication would rob her of their presence.

It was a Sunday morning when news was circulated that her condition had deteriorated overnight, and the medical opinion was that she may not last the day. They gathered around the foot of her bed, and as they stood and shuffled their feet, and the males pocketed their hands, she ran her eye over them focusing intently on her brothers and sisters. She could from long observation see their minds in motion rehearsing well-worn forms of words of relief: "It was a happy release for her," or, "Sure there was no betterment for her."

Her brother David, the eldest sibling, stood at the edge of the crescent-shaped group occasionally glancing out the window. His brown checked shirt was open at the neck, and his sleeves were rolled up, as if ready for a day's work. He worked as a long-haul lorry driver. A chip off the old block—coarse and common with the personality of a waterlogged plank. Social skills he had none. The art of conversation had never colored his life; dialogue was something alien he didn't understand and couldn't master. Not once in her life had she set foot in his home. How strange was that! What impediment prohibited her brother, with the passing of their parents the so-called head of the family, from engaging in everyday ordinary family affairs? God knows she had tried. Every time she had something to celebrate, he and his wife were invited, until she realized she was wasting her time. Yet here he was remote, distant, nothing to say, even now. As she looked at him their eyes met for a moment before he reexamined his boots. *What shaped you? What made you what you are?* She wondered.

She let her eye drift over the gathering at the foot of her bed. It had a kind of delicate choreography all its own. Physical contact was avoided; they moved softly and silently like owls in evening flight, a kind of a soft-shoe shuffle. She wondered who would be the first to leave, the first to blink.

It was then that she felt the feather-like touch on her hand. Turning her head she smiled to acknowledge her eldest sister, Monica. They were close. She remembered as if it was yesterday, the day in the bedroom that they shared, when Monica pressed a birthday present into her hand, a tiny bottle of her favorite Lily of the Valley perfume. It was a secret, just between them. As a family they didn't celebrate birthdays much or anything else for that matter. As she held Monica's hand, she could smell the perfume, sweet, innocent, and feminine. Only now did she realize how complicated it was being a girl then. Monica had mothered them when they were young and growing up. *It was strange,* she thought, *how she and her sisters took after their mother—petite and particular—while the brothers exhibited the traits of their father—coarse and common.* But Monica was more; she was kind, generous, and compassionate.

As the oldest daughter she was assigned child-care duties. In the summer months after all the lunch debris was cleared away and the dishes washed, Monica would take all the younger ones to the seashore. There released from family tensions, she created for them fantasy afternoons filled with fun and laughter.

Six months ago after experiencing bouts of dizziness, Monica was diagnosed with multiple sclerosis. For the moment her condition was not obvious. It was only when walking that her right foot turned slightly inward, signaled all was not as it should be. Life had not been kind to Monica; the man she married hadn't been much of a husband or companion to her. She deserved better. *Best not to dwell on it,* she thought as she gently squeezed Monica's hand. She will not leave; she will be with me to the end. Of that she was absolutely sure.

The sublime dance of the gathering continued through the morning beyond lunch, morphing into a cluster of shuffling penguins. She tried to sip some tea and eat toast but didn't make much of a hand of it. After the dust of lunch had settled and the shuffling feet had stilled a little, she noticed her brother Stephen sitting by himself near the door. Alone all alone, as the song says, on the wave-washed strand, like a piece of discarded flotsam left behind by a grateful sea. He looked tired—ill in fact. He was the third eldest of her brothers and sisters; he was a buyer for a large manufacturing company. His work took him abroad a lot, and that's where he got the taste for alcohol, she thought; after the glamour wears off, one hotel room looks much like another. A taste that grew into an addiction. He was a recovering alcoholic, but he had a softness about him that she always found endearing. As she looked at him now she wondered if he ever had a touch of the learning disabilities. Maybe it was just the way she was seeing him. She scrutinized him for any inkling that he had been drinking earlier in the day, but he gave no sign of it. She knew he would be the first to leave the gathering; he would be the first to go, and someone would have to take him home. He would simply acknowledge her with a wave of his hand and leave. No parting words to slake the desert of their lives.

As the afternoon meandered into early evening, the sun moved silently on its journey across the sky and through her bedside window and bathed her in its gentle light. Her mind was racing. Memory was like a ghost from the past rattling and creaking through the corridors of her mind. She had to control her thoughts, her emotions. Drawing on her meditation skills as she often did in time of stress, she calmed and quieted.

With hooded eyes she again surveyed the gathering. There, prominent center stage, her sister Carol was sitting, knees and feet clamped firmly together, back straight and rigid. Carol was just eighteen months older than her, but she oozed tension, wound up tight like a coiled spring, primed waiting to unleash its stored energy. She felt sorry for her and pity for the placid husband who had to cope with the demons that gnawed like rats on her inner peace. *What shapes us like this*, she wondered? As far as she knew there was no such thing as a behavioral gene; it's not part of our DNA. No, she was satisfied in her own mind that this was learned behavior or induced behavior; something caused it.

Her mother and father when they married had moved into a middle-class 2.2 children family environment. On average her mother produced a child every two years; roughly speaking, she was pregnant for about twenty years full on. *What does that do to a personality petite and particular?* she wondered as she lay feeling her life's energy being squeezed out of her like water squeezed out of a wet sock. She remembered vividly the morning after she had wet the bed when, with a gaggle of her brothers and sisters behind her, mother stood in the middle of the bedroom hands on hips and said to the assembly, "And look at that, another wet bed." She was humiliated, but with the passage of time and much reflection, she came to her understanding. It was quite simple: with nine young children to bring up, washing clothes and bed linen in a jar box with soap and then wringing it through a mangle before getting it on to a washing line to dry, her mother was overwrought.

A hint of a smile again passed unnoticed across her lips, for after she had married and left home she got a letter from Carol telling her that they had just got a washing machine. That's my claim to fame—make that my epitaph, "replaced by a washing machine." She tried to laugh, but it came out as a splutter. Monica fed her water.

She glanced at Carol again, remembering that her drawer in their shared bedroom was the only one with a lock. It was always locked; Carol was very private, none sharing, secretive. *Take note, Carol, before we go our separate ways, you are looking death in the face, my face, and only you can release yourself from your torment; only you can grasp that nettle. I did. I vowed that I would love my children. I would tell them I loved them. I would show that I loved them, and I did. That's why I will die content in the knowledge that love conquers all.*

Her eyes drifted around the gathering, Stephen had said goodbye with a limp wave of his hand. She knew he would be the first to go; he was David's get out of jail card too. David had taken Stephen home; she knew he would not return, not that it mattered now. Carol was getting edgy; she would leave soon too. When she looked around the gathering again, she was gone. Monica had not left her side, caressing her hand and bringing to her mind in word pictures their happy childhoods.

She must have dozed for a while. When she forced open her eyes it was dark outside. Her private room was subtly lit and quiet; the gathering had settled, more chairs had been brought in, and seated conversations were whispered.

She was fighting to the bitter end the thing that was devouring her, piggy in the middle of nine siblings, a tangible link connecting her older and younger siblings, but she doubted if any of them would see her in that light. Her two younger brothers and sisters sat together as a group. They were socially adept, had decent jobs, articulate, yet for two of them their marriages had failed, and the other two it seemed were in no hurry to settle down. She sensed them glancing at their smartphones. They had more pressing matters to attend to. One by one they left until she was surrounded by her own family and Monica.

As Sunday slowly dragged its weary feet toward the advent of Monday, she knew she was drifting in and out of consciousness. Just before Monday surprised Sunday, she came to swimming up from the depths of a dream, believing that she was in her own bed at home. When she forced her eyelids open a little and looked around the remnants of the gathering, she knew exactly where she was.

The sensation of feeling in her feet had abandoned her. It would not be long now; it was coming to take her heart. Pressing the button to increase her medication, she thought, *Je ne regette rien* (I regret nothing). She prayed the words she loved hearing Edith Piaf sing: "Aujourd'hui ca commence avec toi" (Today a new life begins with you—with you).

Drifting slowly away, she recalled *Gitanjali: Song Offerings* ("face-to-face")

> Day after day, O Lord of my life,
> Shall I stand before thee face to face?
> With folded hands, O Lord of all the worlds,
> Shall I stand before thee face to face?

> Under thy great sky in solitude and silence,
> With humble heart shall I stand before thee face to face?
> In this laborious world of thine, tumultuous with toil
> And with struggle, among hurrying crowds
> Shall I stand before thee face to face?

In the early Monday morning she felt she was floating in a shoreless ocean, between earth and sky; her final glance around told her they were all fast asleep except Monica. It had been tough on them. It was time to let go and sail away, vanish into the night like the last glimmer of the setting sun. Closing her eyes, the words of a poem long ago read carried her with colors of indigo, red, green, and azure blue into a meadow of delightful rest.

She died peacefully in her sleep, they all said afterward.

Something for Nothing

His jaw set square, sculpted rivulets of life etched on his weary face, the old man navigated his way slowly through the main doors of the shopping center on a Saturday afternoon. Each step forward was slow, deliberate, and purposeful. He had an old man's stoop, hunched forward as if battling a headwind. Everything about him—his demeanor, bearing, clothes, and scruffiness—suggested destitution. He could be homeless, lost, lonely, bewildered, or bereaved. He could be anything. A black woolen cap, the sort of thing hill walkers and golfers wear in winter, covered his head. Dirty-looking hair hung like rats' tails around his ears and neck. An unkempt dirty gray beard drooped lifelessly under his chin. The full-length, grimy, box-pleated overcoat, perhaps new to him, loosely belted around his middle, covered his long baggy track suit bottoms. Shoddy, discolored, oversize, unlaced guttees sheathed his sockless feet. The trailing ends of the track suit bottoms swept the floor behind him when he slithered forward. A bulging scruffy plastic bag hung from his mitten-covered left hand.

As the shopping center's doors closed quietly behind him, he paused—hesitant confused, unsure of himself. Shoppers milling around gave him a wide berth. After a moment or two looking around, he gathered himself together, shuffled forward sliding one foot after the other against the ebbing consumer tide toward a naturally lit open space, a plaza defined by the shopping center's two anchor stores on his right and left. The plaza was busy, with people mingling, passing through, and some just milling around. It was a meeting place with sparse seating for those wearied of shopping and husbands people-watching, while wives browsed away their togetherness.

The old man shuffled his way into the center of the plaza, stopped, looked around for a little while, and then slowly turned full circle, watching people as they passed, curiously watching him. The ebbing and flowing sea of shoppers rippling through the plaza cautiously rerouted around him, keeping their distance, avoiding contact as if he was somehow contagious. Two men walked past him, and one said to the other, nodding at the old man, "They're everywhere these days." His odd behavior did not go unnoticed by the center's security staff; he wasn't causing any disturbance or annoying anyone, so they too kept their distance, and a watchful eye.

On completion of his strange circling maneuver he opened the plastic bag he was carrying and extracted a crumpled up piece of paper and straightened it out. Then holding it in his mitten-covered right hand between dirty fingers, he offered it to the people passing on his right. No one accepted his offer. The bemused shoppers just eased a little farther away from him. He held the piece of paper aloft for all to see that it was a ten-pound note and again offered it to anyone willing to step forward and take it. Again there were no takers. Holding aloft the tener, he took a step toward what was now a growing cluster of curious onlookers perturbing the flow of shoppers through the plaza. As he stepped toward it, the cluster stepped back in unison away from him hesitant, uncertain, and uneasy. No one, it seemed, dared to forsake the security and comfort of the cluster to take up the old man's offer. His sculpted brow reformed in a deep frown. Then an elderly lady came along, saw him, paused, and rummaged around in her bag. She found her purse, from which she extracted a few coins, and walked toward the old man with hand extended. He shooed her away, but she would not be deterred. She rounded him, dropping the coins into his plastic bag as she passed. Then with a shake of his head, he left those watching nonplussed and shuffled over to the other side of the plaza. He made his offer of a free ten-pound note to the shoppers passing through that side of the plaza. The response was the same. No one wanted or dared to accept from his hand the gift of a ten-pound note. He couldn't give it away. From his gesticulations it was abundantly clear to anyone watching that he had a bagful of tens to give away. Yet the lure of his offer was insufficient to overcome their innate inertia and accept it simply for what it was: something for nothing, a gift. It was the Saturday before Christmas.

Suddenly a little girl let go of her mother's hand, ran up behind him, snatched the ten-pound note from his hand, and with childish glee gifted it to her mother. He turned, saw the child, and smiled broadly, showing his discolored teeth, reached into his plastic bag, pulled out another ten and offered it to her too. The little girl's mother held her close, grudgingly with finger and thumb accepted her prize and with undue haste deposited it in an adjacent waste bin. The pure delight in receiving and giving was wiped from the child's face. On the old man's face sadness banished joy. Ushering the little girl away, her mother produced a packet of antiseptic wipes from her handbag and swabbed the child's hand and her own finger and thumb clean of anything potentially harmful that might have been passed on to them from the crinkled ten-pound note, oblivious of the child's confusion and the old man's displeasure.

For a full hour he tried unsuccessfully to give away his bag of ten-pound notes, and then he put the tenner into his bag, turned, and shuffled slowly out of the shopping center onto the busy street. On his way out he retrieved the tenner from the waste bin, diverting as he went the incoming tide of Saturday afternoon shoppers. In the hour he had spent trying to give away his bagful of money, over four thousand people had ebbed and flowed past him; only one person, a child, had taken the money from his hand.

On the pavement outside, he straightened himself up, removed his woolen cap and beard, took the gum shield out of his mouth, and disrobed revealing a youthful-looking male wearing a T-shirt and jeans. The professionally applied facial prosthetics would be removed later. He combed his hair, took off his guttees, put on shoes, bagged up all his gear, and together with his research team headed back to the university to discuss what they could usefully distill from their afternoon's experiment. The young professor was happy; another little piece of work on the influence of sensory perception on human behavior in different environments was in the bag.

Leaving the university driving home he had a lot to ponder, but he kept his mind on the road, avoided the bus lanes, and stayed within the speed limits. At home over dinner with his wife and daughter, they chatted about what they had been doing all day. When asked about his day he just said that he had been working with some of his students on a little research project, that they had done useful work today, but that there was much more to do before they would have anything useful to publish. In the course of the conversation his daughter told him about the old man in the shopping center giving away ten-pound notes and how she managed to get one. As she told her story she said, "It's usually the other way round, isn't it? Rich people give to the poor. Poor people don't give to better-off people, do they? Nobody except me took the money from him; I was the only one. What do you think of that?" He looked at her for a long moment and smiled before he spoke. "That's a tough question. I'll have to think about that for a minute, but what did you do with the ten-pound note?" His daughter's face clouded a little when she said she gave it to her mother. He thought it best not to pursue that line of inquiry any further.

"You know," he said, "in answer to your big question, you must always remember that things aren't always what they seem. Maybe the old man just had too much money; maybe he had no use for it; maybe he wasn't as old as you think; or maybe he just wanted to make someone a little happier. You know, maybe you made him feel a little happier by taking his money. Have you thought about that?"

His daughter looked at him and smiled.

Stirring the Water

They had eased past the biblical milestone of thee score years and ten a decade earlier, octogenarians content in themselves, still forward looking, enjoying being grandparents. They had grown up a few streets apart on a council estate and had walked the same routes to and from school and had attended the same church, but their paths had never crossed. They met in teenage life, for the first time at a dance in the church hall when Bob was nineteen and Peggy a year older. Their fondness for each other matured, and two years later they were married in their local church, embarking on a journey in life that experience taught them they could have been better prepared for.

Scrolling back in time to the early fifties, Bob dutifully followed in his father's footsteps to become carpenter. Council houses being hard to come by, they lodged for a while with a family friend until they could move up the housing waiting list or perhaps afford a place of their own. Peggy kept on her job and they scrimped and saved what they could until they had enough for a deposit to buy their first home, a small two-up-two-down terrace house. Eventually they acquired a small semidetached house, with gardens front and rear in a more desirable area.

Regular churchgoers, active in parish life, they worked hard bringing up and educating their six children and saw them all through university, forging their chosen careers. It was quite an achievement then, given their working-class background, but it wasn't easy putting six children through university on the combined wages of a tradesman and a part-time shop worker, what with accommodation costs, maintenance, travel, books, and sundries. The price of books, especially the law books, was the straw that almost broke the camel's back, it was fortunate though that they could be handed down. Not that Bob ever thought of himself as a camel—a workhorse maybe but never a camel, no hump on his back, at least not then. With the passage of time they were blessed with the arrival of seven grandchildren, who in many ways kept them on their toes and young at heart. Their eldest grandchild, now a teenager, was preparing to go and experience university life, much to Bob and Peggy's delight. "Tempus fugit," Bob in reflective mood often would say to Peggy as they observed each of their grandchildren growing up before their eyes.

Looking back he recalled an evening when he came home tired after a long day's work. The house was quiet; Peggy had all the children washed and in bed for the night. Bob had barely sat down to the meal Peggy had prepared for him, when she announced in her quiet serious way that she had decided to take on another part-time job. Without thinking, Bob mumbled a "What for?"

"Because we need the money, Bob," Peggy responded knowing full well he knew why but didn't want to acknowledge why. Bob stared at the food on the table before him in silence, as an overwhelming feeling of inadequacy and hopelessness engulfed him. He was working ten hours a day six days a week, and Peggy was making every penny stretch as far as it could stretch. The food getting cold in front of him didn't yield any answers to their dilemma, but it gave him time to think, set his feelings aside, and accept Peggy's decision knowing full well the demands it would make on her. He knew she was right; they needed some "readies" to get them through their present difficulties, and then all would be well, he hoped! They had always resisted the temptation to borrow money, determined to stay debt free. He didn't like the idea of his wife having two jobs, though there was no shame attached to it, but he would hide his dislike as best he could and would do everything possible to lessen the burden on Peggy. Together as they always did, they combined their energies to resolve as he saw it their temporary difficulties and move on.

Despite occasional financial anxieties, they never failed to honor their weekly donation at church on Sundays. The weekly offertory promise collection was introduced the year after they were married as a means of planned giving—one envelope collection replacing all the other bits and pieces of the tin plate collections that had gone before. Planned gifting, as it was promoted at the time, guaranteed church revenues by securing promised single weekly donations from all wage-earning parishioners. Promises made, promises kept, he remembered, was the promoters' mantra.

Regardless of his involvement in the parish community, faith didn't come easily to Bob; he struggled with it. Often in church he would sit and look up at the stained glass image of the crucified Christ above the altar wondering, *Why did you do it? Are you really the son of God? Am I truly a son of God? Who is God anyway?* It was all a big mystery to him. He could, having left school at fourteen, get his head around the complex geometry of roofs and timber stairs, but it was hard to understand all the stuff drummed into him in school about God, three persons in one, from the content of a penny catechism. The questions that agitated in the recesses of his mind were in the Sunday service homilies, described as mysteries and left hanging without explanation. He knew he should have read more and sought more enlightenment. How could he when he was literally working his fingers to the bone to keep family and home together. His notion of faith, however, was all embracing inclusive and full of hope. All he sought was to understand his place in the scheme of things and his relationship with his God. In that sense his faith was truly simple, unfettered by knowledge of theology and canon law.

Peggy was quite wonderfully different; she had no doubts at all and had a ready explanation for everything, no matter what, firmly rooted in her notion of a loving God. Naïve, some might have said, or just a simple faith. Peggy attended church regularly, Bob less frequently. "My cathedral," he was often heard to say, "is early mornings on a roof between earth and sky, the beauty of creation in plain sight all around me." Bob knew he could never fully understand the mystery of life; because he could not fully understand it didn't mean that he couldn't believe, but it never rested easy with him.

Their faith—their belief—was severely tested when their firstborn was killed in a motor vehicle accident abroad. Devastated, they couldn't believe that life around them just seemed to carry on as if nothing had happened. Much later, when reason found its voice, they acknowledged the reality of life; accidents were a common occurrence, and it was their turn this time in the roulette of living. Together with much mind- and soul-searching they somehow slowly clawed back the threadbare roots of life again and gradually reconciled themselves in faith to their loss. The demands of family routine helped, but there was always a void, an emptiness that even faith at times found hard to fill. The inarticulate voices of their minds and hearts wondered why God allowed such disasters to happen. It was something they would ponder for the rest of their lives. Many years would pass before Bob could bring himself even to speak of it without distress.

Fast-forward six decades. Bob was sitting in the kitchen when he heard the letter box rattle followed by a thump as something heavy met the floor. He could see what it was before he got to the door; they were the recipients of a new set of hand-delivered church donation envelopes. It was that time of the year again. He picked it up, sat down at the kitchen table, and casually perused the little box. Over the years since it was first introduced it had grown significantly in envelope-holding capacity. The inaugural box had contained only fifty-two white donation envelopes, one for each week, issued to every participating wage earner in the parish. The covenant between parishioners and parish administrators was that planned giving meant committing to a promised donation every week. The envelopes in the box just delivered were all the colors of the rainbow, it seemed, and there were many more than the inaugural fifty-two in the box. Intrigued, Bob emptied the box and counted the envelopes, he reckoned that on about thirty Sundays in the upcoming liturgical church year the congregation would be expected to make two envelope donations. He sat back in his chair to digest the significance of what had tumbled out of the innocuous little box just launched through his letter box. Year on year some diocesan administrator, without as much as a by your leave, was increasing the number of envelopes in the box to boost income extracted from parishioners. Bob thought back to the times when he and Peggy were cash-strapped; they worked longer, harder, to make up what was needed to make ends meet. He supposed cash-strapped church administrators worked harder too, by increasing the number of donation envelopes issued to each parishioner.

Bob and Peggy had scrimped and saved for their retirement. They weren't well off; they had enough to provide for their latter years, and what they didn't need they were in the process of giving away. Their reasoning was simple. Their respective pasts were getting longer and their futures shorter. They had few if any needs and even fewer wants and abhorred hoarding. They would have welcomed parental monies if their parents had any to give them when they most needed it. Everything in life, they had learned, was a balance. If there was no love in the home, what good was money? Without love, truth, compassion, and self-esteem as their foundation, family life would have been stunted. For them the true purpose of having money was to liberate love and encourage the bud of generosity to burst and blossom. He wondered, looking at the array of envelopes on the table in front of him, what exactly the needs of their church were that necessitated an additional thirty weekly envelope donations from them. They wondered because no one had ever bothered to tell them; they were just expected, it seemed, to donate on demand.

He was still ruminating when he heard Peggy calling that it was time to go to church. Lost in thought, he'd almost forgotten it was Sunday. Before leaving the house he suffered Peggy's predictable interrogation. "Have you got the donation and the monthly stipend envelopes for the collections?"

"Yes," Bob dutifully responded, "and the money for the door collection on the way in, and the money for the parish bulletin, not that it's worth a penny, and the money for the poor box. Is there anything I've missed'?

"No," said Peggy. "We've no one to light candles for today, thanks be to God."

As they were walked to church, Bob saw that Peggy had a plastic bag with her, but he passed no remarks; he had learned long ago not to question Peggy's doings when it came to churchgoing.

They attended the church where their families had worshipped for generations. They knew where they had sat with their parents on Sundays. If only these walls could talk, they could tell stories; Bob put the intrusive thought away—better to focus on the here and now than on mindless musing.

Having acknowledged the door collection, purchased the information-challenged bulletin—one to each family was the allocation—Bob waited while Peggy deposited her plastic bag among the other plastic bags and cardboard boxes of foodstuffs donated to the town's burgeoning food bank for distribution to those in need, and then they took their usual pew.

The warning bell announced the entrance procession. *The entire world's a stage*, Bob thought as his mind tuned Shakespearean again.

The first reading addressed the futility of life; vanity of vanities! *Omnia Vanitas.* An image of his sister prizing her feet into high heel shoes two sizes too small captioned with his mother's rebuke, "Ah, sure, pride feels no pain," scurried across his mind's eye. The second reading implored the listeners to look and see what was above and beyond worldly endeavors. *More like it*, Bob thought. *More my kind of thing.* He had no problem putting to death evil designs; he felt he hadn't acquired any yet, and greed was alien to his nature. He was never one to acquire and flaunt possessions for possessions' sake; in fact, the fewer possessions he had the better he felt. Motor cars and like status symbols were not for him. A bad thought crossed his mind, maybe a little pride was flaunting itself, but he swished it away as he would a fly.

As soon as the homily began, Bob knew that he and the preacher were in sync, singing off the same hymn sheet, as they say. The gist of the homily was about how possessions can take over people's lives, by becoming an end in themselves to the extent that sight of their real value is lost. The constant bombardment by way of junk mail and aggressive advertising of things people didn't really need or want was emphasized. The focus on personal greed and avarice made Bob feel a little edgy—uncomfortable. Corporate greed was not mentioned—left out, overlooked, and ignored—notwithstanding the activities of banks and hedge funds and corporate pursuit of maximum profits and so on in an era of austerity. *This omission,* Bob thought, *against a backcloth of austerity and a significant increase in the number of donation envelopes; can we really all be in this together?* A chill slowly wrapped itself around him.

Coming into church he had acknowledged the door collection in the usual way, paid for a parish news sheet, would donate to two envelope collections, and on the way out would put something in the poor box for the needy. The latter he had to because Peggy would be at the door holding the box accepting the donations; there was no escape.

The priest, after exchanging greetings with exiting parishioners, reentered the church and literally bumped into Bob. Polite apologies were uttered; Bob, taking the opportunity of the chance encounter, asked him why he hadn't mentioned corporate greed in his homily. Smiling the question away, the priest tried to ease past, but Bob arresting his flight and said, "Do you not think that in this age of austerity, when some 60 percent of people are having difficulty paying their bills, with a food bank just around the corner, a food bank depository in church, that two envelope collections today is a bit much?"

Without even a hint of a hesitation the priest responded, "We need the money," and with that parting shot, still smiling, he strode purposely away, leaving Bob's mouth hanging open like a barn door on one hinge. *He doesn't get it,* Bob thought, *otherwise he wouldn't have said what he did, or perhaps he just forgot in his desire to be rid of me that the second collection today was the monthly stipend for the priests of the parish.*

What did he mean "we"? wondered Bob as he sat down in the pew waiting for Peggy to unload her poor box. *Was it the parish?* Couldn't possibly be, according to the annual income and expenditure information delivered annually from the pulpit. When the planned giving scheme was introduced many decades ago, only fifty-two white parish offertory envelopes were in the box he was allocated then. In the box he was looking at before coming to church, there were still fifty-two of the same white parish donation envelopes, and donations had increased in real terms. No, he couldn't have meant the parish. *Did the "we" then*, Bob wondered, *mean the clergy?* He knew without even thinking about it that it couldn't be because previously four clergy serving the parish were supported from donations in the twelve yellow monthly stipend envelopes like the one he put on the plate today. But the complement of clergy servicing the parish had been reduced from four to one, and the monthly stipend donations had kept pace with inflation. That account must be in the black. No it wasn't that. It had to be something else, or it was just a knee jerk reaction when caught unawares. Did the "we" refer to the institution—the organization? *The diocese, that had to be it*, he thought, but he wasn't sure, though he had long suspected that it had been top-slicing parish income.

Back home at the kitchen table, cup of tea to hand, he emptied the box of envelopes delivered earlier and spread them out before him, setting aside the fifty-two white weekly and twelve monthly stipend yellow offering ones. Then he counted five pink voluntary collection envelopes for spring, autumn, New Year's, Easter, and Christmas. Bob took a deep breath as he digested the subtlety in the choice and use of the word *voluntary* on the face of these envelopes.

He then turned his attention to the remaining bundle of green envelopes spread out on the table. There were a dozen of them on which the word *voluntary* was not used, suggesting by omission compulsory. Leafing through them, he discovered that the monies donated in these envelopes were not destined for parish use; they were for designated good causes such as the Diocesan Church Fund, Diocesan Pastoral Services, Bishops Commissions, and Education Of Diocesan Students. Bob realized that he was wrong. The diocese was not just top-slicing the parish funds; it was using parishes as money orchards that could be regularly harvested. *Who said money doesn't grow on trees?* Bob started to giggle at the thought and then laughed out loud.

What he now understood was that the original covenant for a single weekly collection had been augmented by twelve monthly stipend collections, five voluntary seasonal collections, and twelve diocesan good causes collections, and that out of eighty-one envelope collections, only five were labeled voluntary. He wondered why. On twenty-nine Sundays in the church calendar year, parishioners would experience two envelope collections. By a simple process of envelope screening, Bob had determined that the "we" referred to the institution. It needed the money, and a Jesuit solution to the problem had been employed—don't invalidate the covenant, just massage it to advantage. The question was still valid. What was the money actually needed and subsequently used for? That was what he was unclear about.

He cleared the table for lunch, during which he regaled Peggy with his encounter with the priest, implying that he might pursue it with him next week. Peggy slowly arranged her knife and fork on either side of her plate, looked him straight in the eye, and said, "You'll only stir the water, Bob."

To which he responded, "Maybe it needs stirred a bit."

Peggy said nothing; silence stretched and yawned until she said, "A gentle stir will only cause a few ripples, but stirring and stirring will create turbulence, and the water won't get any clearer; best leave it as is, and anyway we could always adjust our donating." Practical as ever, Peggy's solution was that they just shape their donating to reflect the pastoral care they received, including something toward church maintenance.

Together as always they addressed the issue in a commonsense way by considering the end use of donations by envelope color. In the end they decided there were two possible courses of action to take; they could reduce their weekly envelope contributions by a factor of four, since they now had only one priest instead of four, or they could simply pay for the service they received. They mulled it over for a while and decided not to adjust their weekly white envelope donation. They had signed up for that, had maintained their support through hard times and good, and they would not default. The twelve stipend collections they would reduce to three; after all there was only one priest in the parish now. They would consider the other seventeen envelope collections on a one-by-one basis; after all no one had taken up a collection to help them educate their six children. No, they would decide what they would in conscience support, putting always the poor and needy first.

Sitting by the fireside that evening, Bob thought of the day many years ago when Peggy told him she was taking a second job because they needed the money. At least they knew then what they needed the money for and how they would go about earning it.

Hard times come again no more, he thought, momentarily forgetting about austerity.

Street Theater

All the world's a stage, and all the men and women merely players; they have their exits and their entrances, and one man in his time plays many parts. These are the words Shakespeare put into the mouth of Jacques in his play *As You Like It*. The same sentiment could be expressed in another way; all the stage is a world and all the players merely men, women, and children who perform their unscripted dramas, undirected to full effect in kitchen houses and on street corners. Improvisation happens naturally; their dramas unfold before our unseeing eyes. Drama is the thing that makes the play, and it happens every day all around us.

Grainne O'Malley had just turned twenty one; she was single, unattached, very attractive in all respects, and had many suitors but none that had as yet fired her imagination. She was the transport manager for a local but substantial road haulage company that conducted its business all across Europe. Grainne was good at her job, had an aptitude for it, and was computer literate; logistical complexities didn't faze her. She was a very good problem solver and organizer. More than that, she had a personality to complement that endeared her to everyone she worked with, including and particularly the long-distance lorry drivers. She understood the loneliness of the long-distance lorry driver and openly empathized.

Away from work she was actively involved in the local dramatic society. Although she had performed on stage, her interest and forte was stage management. She loved it. In every way it showcased her confidence in what she was doing, her ability and reliability, and her organizational attributes to great effect. To the dramatic society she was a treasure. Each year, spring and autumn, the dramatic society put on two public performances in addition to many other activities such as public readings of plays and various outreach activities. Tonight was the last night of their spring production; it had all gone well—no major hiccups on or off stage, and the production enjoyed very receptive audiences. Grainne had accrued some holidays that she was obliged to take or lose them; as the final curtain closed, she was looking forward to a long midweek break in Dublin, her destination of choice. The party after the final performance was intoxicatingly merry; everyone was in high spirits, tinged with relief and disappointment that the run had ended.

Next morning Grainne, bright and bushy-tailed, was on board the early train for Dublin. She had booked into Wynn's Hotel on Abbey Street. She would arrive too early to book in proper, but that didn't matter as her overnight bag was light; she packed only the bare necessities. She always stayed at Wynn's Hotel when in Dublin; it was very central, and places she wanted to visit, including the theaters, were within easy walking distance. The building itself had history, was full of character, and oozed hospitality. But most of all she looked forward to the cooked breakfasts, especially the eggs benedict. The hotel also had a cozy bar where guests could relax in the evenings and enjoy conversation without having to speak loudly to make themselves heard. To get to Wynn's from the station was easy; the Dublin tram route designers had sited a tram stop conveniently outside the hotel.

On arrival in Dublin she decided she would take the tram to Grafton Street, get off, and proceed on foot to Bewley's Oriental Café for morning coffee. It was another of her favorite haunts. Looking out the train window, she noticed rain spots appearing on the glass. It didn't matter; it would take more than that to dampen her enthusiasm; anyway she had a fold-up brolly in her bag if needed. After morning coffee in Bewley's, she would explore Grafton Street, bottom to top, and finish with a few exploratory circuits of St. Stephen's Green before booking in at Wynn's Hotel and readying herself for the Abbey Theatre later in the evening. So first day planned, more or less, she settled back in her seat, closed her eyes and ears to the world around her, and relaxed.

In Dublin she proceeded as planned: boarded the tram, drifted contentedly past Wynn's Hotel, dismounted close to Grafton Street, and made her way to Bewley's Oriental Café. As soon as she walked in she was transported into another world; the mingling aromas of coffees teased her sense of smell, and the magnificent stained glass windows filled her eyes; she was totally absorbed in the moment. She felt she was rubbing shoulders, connecting with some of the giants of the arts in Ireland, feeling privileged and unworthy at the same time. Joyce, she remembered had mentioned this very place in *The Dubliners*. Somewhat awestruck, she found a table to sit and consider what the menu offered. Grainne loved the place—the old world atmosphere, the pace of its life, and its clientele. She didn't really need to look at the menu because she was going to have what she called the house coffee, a double espresso with hints of pineapple, lime, and brown sugar, but her eye had slipped to the dessert menu and the Bewley's classic, The Mary Cake, a chocolate mousse with an apricot center on an almond and hazelnut sponge. Unconsciously licking her lips, she pondered, *Should I, or should I not?* She decided not, leaving her options open, possibly to return for Bewley's Café Theatre for an invigorating lunchtime experience as well as a spot of lunch perhaps. As she sat long over her coffee, people watching, her mind flicked through remembered remnants of Durcan's poem "Bewley's Oriental Café, Westmoreland Street." The lines "It is as chivalrous as it is transcendental, to be sitting in Bewley's Oriental Café," summed up completely, comprehensively, how happy and relaxed she felt. Preparing with some regret to take her leave, the last few lines of the poem galloped into her head: "Keeping an eye on his things, and old ladies with thousands of loaves of brown bread under their palaeolithic oxters." She started laughing at the thought, drawing attention from two such well-dressed ladies sitting at an adjoining table. She excused herself to no one in particular and walked out onto Grafton Street.

It was midmorning, but already Grafton Street was buzzing with pedestrian activity; there was excitement in the air, and she could feel its current surging through her. Voices milling around her spoke in French, German, Spanish, and other languages she didn't know. It was a shifting complex pattern of color, sound, and movement, and it was mesmerizing. The flower sellers had their stalls out packed to the gunnels with flowers for every occasion scenting the air to the delight of the passersby. Street musicians entertained, artists made landscapes and portraits on paving slabs with colored crayons, a mime artist dressed as Spiderman pretended to climb an imaginary glass wall; Grainne absorbed it all. As she moved up the street toward St. Stephen's Green, she came upon a series of what might be described as street performers, the ones that perch on boxes or pedestals to elevate themselves, dressed to mimic someone of note, freeze in a characteristic pose, and make an exaggerated gesture in response to a donation. A few had added sound tracks of mechanical and other noises to amplify their attraction. She looked them over each one in turn but did not reach for her purse; they reminded her of mechanical toys—automatons. People behaving like machines didn't impress her; they lacked personality. Before she realized it she had reached the top of Grafton Street; across the busy road in front of her, St. Stephen's Green was her next port of call.

She waited until the traffic calmed and then sprinted across the road toward the majestic archway entrance to the park. Pausing to get her breath back, she looked back down the narrow pedestrian thoroughfare she had just left, taking in the ebbing and flowing tide of pedestrian traffic with all its sights, sounds, textures, and colors.

Turning to enter the park, she saw an old woman standing just beyond the archway. She was bent over, dressed entirely in black—long ankle-length black shirt, black blouse, black shoes, and a black fringed wraparound shawl draped over her head covering her shoulders and back and knotted at her waist—what she remembered her mother called an Irish mantle. With her black-gloved right hand she leaned on a blackthorn stick; in her other black-gloved hand she held a tin mug. Grainne wondered if she was another automaton but thought she was a bit off the commercial track for that. As she looked at her more closely, she wondered who she was and what she was doing. Did she need help? Was she homeless? Was she confused?

Slowly she found herself feeling concerned for the old woman, whatever was troubling her if anything didn't matter. All that mattered at that moment was, Did she need help? *What can I do?* Grainne asked herself. She emptied her purse of what cash she had; it was all coinage; all day she had used her credit card, but it was the best she could do. So fist full of coins, she made toward the outstretched hand holding the tin mug. She whispered to the bowed head, "Sorry, this is the best I can do for now." The bowed head didn't move. When she dropped her handful of coins into the tin mug, the bowed head snapped to attention, the eyes momentarily smiled a thank you, and then suddenly the mouth opened and from somewhere deep inside a voice started shrieking like an animal in pain. The shrieking went on and on, repeating something like "I'm not a beggar. I don't need your money or your kindness, you stupid girl," over and over again. The old woman kept on shrieking, but strangely Grainne was the only one who seemed to hear her. No one else was paying her any attention; they just kept going about their business as if nothing untoward was happening. Then threateningly she raised her stick and threw her tin mug at Grainne, scattering its contents over the ground. Grainne was frightened and didn't know what to do. She thought briefly about trying to reason with the old woman, but when she moved toward her, the stick was brandished like a club. That's when Grainne took to her heels and ran. She could still hear the old woman shrieking as she ran, and it was only when she stopped hearing the shrieking that she stopped running. Out of breath, confused, disorientated, she didn't know how to find her way out of the park and back to her hotel. She rounded a bend in the path she had ran along, almost colliding with a young farm hand leading a plow horse harnessed up for work. She stopped and asked him for directions. He kindly pointed out the way for her to go; she didn't tarry on her way back to Wynn's hotel. She needed time to clear her head.

At the hotel she registered, got the keys to her room, considered having a drink in bar, thought better of it, and went to her room to freshen up. As she relaxed lying on the bed after a very hot bath, she pondered over what had actually happened. When she registered at the hotel it was five o'clock in the early evening. Where had all the day gone? She couldn't get her head around it. She reasoned with herself; she had partied albeit carefully the night before; she was up very early this morning, tea and toast for breakfast; trained her way to Dublin; had coffee in Bewley's intending to go back there for lunch, which she didn't; and hadn't eaten anything all day. Perhaps she was just overtired, in need of sustenance, and her mind was playing tricks on her. With those thoughts she cheered herself up and readied herself for the theater later, after she visited her favorite restaurant in Dublin first for something substantial to eat.

Grainne had splashed out on a good seat in the Abby Theatre just down the road from her hotel, arrived early, got herself a gin and tonic at the bar, ordered her interval refreshment, found a vantage point, and settled to observe the entrance parade of patrons for the evening performance of *Sive*. It was a play she had long wanted to see but somehow at every available opportunity something came up that required her attention, and she missed out. The plot she read in the program told the story of the illegitimate eighteen-year-old Sive who lived with her uncle Mike and his wife, Mena, and Nanna Mike's mother. The local matchmaker convinces Mena to agree to the marriage of Sive to a rich but haggard old man, for a fee of course. Sive is in love with a young plowman who unfortunately is deemed unsuitable. Distraught at being forced into a marriage she did not relish, Sive, dressed in white, in the dead of night runs out of the house in despair into the bog and is later found dead in a bog hole by the lad she loved. It was only when she had taken her allotted seat that on closer reading of the program that she discovered that the playwright, John B. Keane, had named the play *Sive* in honor of his sister, Shiela, by using the Gaelic form of the name. Grainne smiled to herself as she read that; her middle name was Shiela. Maybe she should change her middle name to Sive. Who would know? Her initials would remain the same. *Why not?* she thought as the house lights dimmed, the patrons quieted, and the curtains parted. She was totally immersed in the play; engrossed and enthralled, mixed emotions permeated her being, but most of all she felt compassion for Sive.

The play ended to rapturous applause. She sat transfixed as the theater emptied its patrons out into the welcoming Dublin night, at one with Sive—feeling her pain, helplessness, and utter desperation. The theater staff was about their business of tidying up in and around the vacated seats when she forced herself out of her seat and left. Occupied in deep thought, she made her way slowly back up Abby Street to her hotel.

It was quite late, but she had nothing pressing tomorrow. *So perhaps a nightcap might help me to relax,* she thought. One or two people were still in the bar; she took a stool by the bar and perched up, set her little clutch bag and theater program on the bar counter, caught the barman's eye, and asked for a large Courvoisier with no ice. Her drink was set up on a bar mat accompanied by a little tray of nibbles. Raising the brandy glass to her nose, she sniffed the characteristic bouquet, sipped the amber nectar, and felt the warming fluid caressing her anguished thoughts. She had without realizing it quickly sipped her glass empty, and when she glanced around, the bar too was empty; the barman was gone. She was considering bed when a different barman appeared, nodded at her glass, and said, "Same again?" Nodding her assent, she considered him; he was older than the other barman, middle-aged and gray-haired, with a gentle sunny personality. He served her drink in a fresh glass, which to her glance seemed more generous than the first, and chatted as barmen and barbers do with regulars and others. It never occurred to her to wonder how he knew what she was drinking. As she sipped her drink she talked about the play she had been to see—the production, the set, the lighting, the atmosphere in the theater, what it was all about, and the tragic ending. He listened attentively until she had finished. "You do know," he said, "the playwright's sister didn't want the play to be named after her." He looked at her for a moment and then continued. "It wasn't just the play; she didn't want to be emotionally connected or associated with the unhappy girl and her sorrowful end. That play is a bit like Shakespeare's *Macbeth*; strange things are said to have happened when it has been performed."

Intrigued, Grainne then told him all about her encounter with the old woman in St. Stephen's Green earlier in the day and how she eventually found her way out of the park. When she had talked herself out, he said, "What do you make of it, then?" When she didn't answer he continued. "Maybe she was just looking for a bit of kindness, some understanding; after all you did say she whispered 'thank you.' There could have been a demon locked inside her that didn't want released. Your act of kindness may have forced it out. Have you thought of that?" Well, she hadn't; she was so afraid that she ran for her life. Then he said, "By the way, there wouldn't be a plowman with a horse harnessed for plowing in the park; it wouldn't be allowed." She looked up puzzled but grateful to him for listening to her and for his kind words; that's when she noticed the name tag on his left breast: John. D. She wondered if his surname was Dempsey, Doherty, Donaldson, or what, and made to ask him, but he was no longer there. She emptied her glass and went to bed.

Next morning Grainne was up and about later than usual, skeptical if not a little befuddled. Freshened by a very hot shower, she was determined to enjoy her eggs benedict breakfast. She had intended to visit the Writers Museum and the National Library today, but was drawn back to Grafton Street. Walking slowly, deliberately taking her time, she retraced her steps of yesterday, including coffee in Bewley's. Some the street artists, musicians, and street performers were different, but she expected that because she knew that pitches were licensed and rotated among licensees. The atmosphere, colors, and sounds were much the same as they were yesterday, with lots of people milling about. When she reached the top of the street and across toward St. Stephen's Green, the old woman dressed in black was gone. In her place in a similar pose stood a young woman dressed entirely in white. Grainne stood stock still, fixed to the spot, momentarily paralyzed, physically and mentally. Bemused, she backed away uncertain of what to do. Then the words the barman had spoken in conversation last night returned, encouraging and challenging her to go forward. At the nearest flower stall, she bought a bespoke bunch of red and white roses, which she felt embodied everything good she felt about the young girl Sive in the play she had seen last night: purity, innocence, gentleness, and suffering. She went back to the top of the street, waited for traffic to stop, and walked with slow determination toward the girl in white. Standing before her, she bowed her head and said, "For you with love." The girl in white looked at her and said, "This is the nicest thing that has happened to me all day." With that they parted. Grainne, walking through the park, wondered why she had done what she just did and could find no answer, but she was glad she did and felt the better for it.

She didn't do the things she had planned for the day, but it didn't really matter. They could wait; they weren't going anywhere. Late afternoon drifted through evening into night. In Temple bar she found a nice quiet restaurant and settled in for a long enjoyable dinner with a nice French red wine.

Later, back in her hotel, she ventured into the bar, perched on the same bar stool as before and asked for a Courvoisier with no ice. She was served by the first barman she had met the night before, her drink accompanied by a tray of nibbles. When she asked about the other barman, John D, she was told that no one by that name worked there; she described him, to be told again that no one of that description or name worked there. Perplexed, she decided to pursue the matter no further, finished her drink, and went to bed.

Awake early next morning completely refreshed, all cares and concerns erased from her mind, she was looking forward to a relaxing day in her favorite place. She breakfasted late again on eggs benedict again. Why not? She would never cook it at home. Then feeling happy in herself, she left the hotel headed for O'Connell Street, crossed O'Connell Bridge spanning the river Liffey, and went up Westmoreland Street until she was standing before the arched entrance to Trinity College. There she paused, drinking it all in and savoring the hallowed atmosphere. Walking through the entrance, which is part of Regent House, she paused and looked into what may have once been a doorkeeper's room at some time, recalling the lunchtime plays performed there by fellow students before ten or twelve patrons maximum; that's all the space could hold. Memories came flooding back. *It's where I probably found my love of theater*, she thought. She moved on but not too far; she had to pop into the chapel, it was a must, as was the library with its long room and the Book of Kells. She was here for the day, she knew. She had spent four very happy years here, and she was grateful for it. As the afternoon wore on, she found herself walking around the northern perimeter of the college; she decided to leave the campus for a little while and headed up Kildare Street, turning right onto St. Stephen's Green North making for the arched entrance to St. Stephen's Green. She had to see if they were there, either of them—the old woman in black or the young girl in white. Neither of them was there. She felt relieved, glad; she didn't know precisely why, couldn't explain it if asked to, but she was just happy. Back inside Trinity College, she was sitting on the steps in front of the chapel enjoying the late afternoon sun watching people going about their business, admiring the iconic campanile, a favorite meeting place in her student days, when someone said, "Fancy meeting you here!" Taken unawares, she turned slightly, squinting into the setting sun and eventually recognizing one of her old classmates. "John, fancy meeting you here," she blurted out. "I'm up in Dublin for a couple of days on a bit of business. What are you doing down here?" It was the language of the past; when you're from the north you go down to Dublin, but when you're from the south you go up to Dublin. They chatted for a while, then, since they had no plans for the evening, they arranged to meet up again for dinner.

To cut a long story short, Grainne is now Mrs. John Deane, living in Dublin, and is very happy. Serendipity perhaps, but there is drama all around us—micro, macro, every day, everywhere. What's a life without a little drama? Drama's the thing.

The Vikings Are Coming

They had spent the morning at Sandy Bay beach just a stone's throw from where they lived. Freddie, Bob's seven-year-old son, happily played in the sand designing, building, and rebuilding castle fortifications against invaders from the sea. He had learned about the Vikings in school—how they came in their longboats from a place far away—they had become for him a bit of an obsession. Other boys his age were into football or dinosaurs, but Freddie's thing was Vikings. Eventually satisfied his fortifications could withstand any Viking assault, he flopped down beside his dad, a question already formed and primed to launch like a torpedo on his unsuspecting father. "What's that?" he asked, pointing to the tall stone tower at the tail end of the causeway sticking out into the sea. Bob, knowing his son's young mind was fermenting like the grape juice he had bubbling away in his roof space, with notions of Vikings, thought he'd add a bit of rainbow to color his son's thoughts. "Auch, that," he said. "That's the watchtower folk built hundreds of years ago to warn the people that lived here when the Vikings were coming." Freddie's mouth opened wide like a farm gate on market day.

Looking down at the castle fortifications he had just built, minus a watchtower, he sheepishly asked, "What's a watchtower?" knowing full well what it was. "Well, you know the Vikings came here raiding in their longboats hundreds of years ago and stole stuff from the folk that lived here," his father explained. "They were fierce, big warriors; they killed folk and took young ones away to be their slaves. The tower was built, you see, for the folk to keep watch so that they would know if the Vikings were coming back again."

"How did they do that?" Freddie asked, a wee frown wrinkling his virgin brow.

"In shifts," his father answered, immediately regretting the words before they left his mouth, knowing full well that he had invited another question.

"What are shifts?" Freddie unsurprisingly wanted to know.

Bob warmed to the task now and thinking he could introduce some math into the conversation said. "It's like taking turns doing things, like in games; they kept watch day and night, and with twelve hours in each day and night, that's twenty-four hours, and divide by four you get," "six" Freddie, fully engaged, excitedly shouted out. "But how would they see at night? They'd have no electric," he asked, his wee face creased in a frown. Slightly on the back foot, Bob explained that they would use a torch at night to climb the—he almost said spiral but realized his folly in time—winding stairs until they got to the top of the tower, and then they would sit and keep watch until their shift was done.

"Where would they get the batteries for the torches?" Freddie wanted to know.

"Not that kind of torch, Freddie." Bob was about to say their torches were made with rushes and tallow in those times but realized that if he did he wouldn't be able to quell Freddie's insatiable curiosity, so he continued, "They had candles fixed on the end of wooden poles."

Freddie looked at him as if he had a couple of slates loose. "They'd sit up there all night by themselves staring out a window. They couldn't read nor nothing. What did they do all night? What did they do when they needed to go to the toilet? And how would they keep the window clean?" he asked.

Things were getting a bit tricky. Freddie's questions were coming at him thick and fast like midges at the moss on a summer's night. Bob would have to distract him, otherwise he would go on and on with the whys and the wherefores.

"They didn't have glass windows in those days son," he explained. "It would have been a wee opening in the wall they could look out of, and if they saw the Vikings coming, they had a rope tied to a bell they could ring to warn the people. The men and women took turns watching at night, and during the day the boys and girls watched so that the men and women could do their work. At night the women would do their knitting and stuff like that, you know, stuff they could do in the dark, like your mother watching TV, knitting, and talking at the same time. The men would sharpen their swords, mend nets, and stuff like that."

Seeing another question germinating in Freddie's mind, Bob quickly carried on. "You know that Freddie is the shortened version of Frederick, a Viking name."

Freddie's eyes lit up like a beacon. Bob went on to explain that the Vikings' name for Larne Lough, where they were, was Ulfreksfjord, which later became Wulfrickford, and that from the two you get Frederick. He wrote the names on a piece of paper, showing his son the connections. Freddie's eyes shone like the shafts of light from nearby lighthouse over the sea on a dark night. His father inwardly dreaded trying to explain to his wife, Marjorie, why he was filling the child's head with this nonsense. "You're fortunate," Bob carried on regardless, "there's not that many Viking names around anymore." Feeling full of the tale, he foolishly didn't quit when he was ahead. "The only other one I can think of is the old castle we went to see a while ago, Olderfleet Castle. Olderfleet is a Viking name, you know."

Freddie burst his father's balloon when he innocently asked, "Why did they never finish building it, Dad?" Too late Bob realized the error of his ways but quick on his feet concocted another story.

Freddie sat knees tucked up under his chin, eyes fixed on his father's face, poised and waiting like a cat eyeing a mouse. There was no get out of jail card coming from Freddie. Bob would just have to wing it. "Your grandfather told me the way of it," Bob said, and looking at Freddie as only a father could, went on to tell the story of why the Olderfleet castle was never finished.

He told Freddie about the discovery of the Viking warrior's grave at the side of Larne Lough many years ago. The Viking warrior killed in a raid was buried by his fellow Vikings, but the warrior had brought his young son along for the experience, thinking it would be no bother. The watchers in the tower saw them coming and raised the alarm. The Viking raiders were surprised by the brave men from the villages and were driven back into the sea. The Viking's son got separated from his father when the fighting started. He hid in the whin bushes until it got dark. In the morning the Vikings' longboat was gone. The boy was alone, far away from home, among strangers. He was lost and afraid. Lucky for him he was found by an old woman who took him up to her isolated cabin in the Glen of 'O,' now called Gleno, and reared him as her son. He grew up to be a big strong man with flaming red hair and piercing blue eyes. She knew he was a Viking and called him Alfred after the Viking king Ulfrek, but locally he was called Alfie. He was the local builder—had hands for anything, didn't overcharge, and left good work wherever he wrought.

One day Alfie was sent for by the local chieftain, who wanted a castle built. When he was there, Alfie set eyes for the first time on the chieftain's daughter, Emir, and was smitten. Emir looked at Alfie, and they both knew it was love at first sight. The chieftain saw it too. When Alfie asked him for his daughter's hand in marriage, he agreed on one condition: that Alfie would build his new castle in six months. Alfie agreed, also with one condition: that he would not be overlooked doing the work and that no one would visit the site until the castle was complete. He started building the castle and worked day and night at it. During the day he would plan, arrange, organize materials, and all those sorts of things, but it was at night that all the heavy lifting seemed to be done. In the morning, walls would have as if by magic risen out of the ground to greet the rising sun.

Alfie had a secret. He had a little earthenware bottle that his father had given him for safekeeping. In the bottle his father kept a captured Viking fairy. At night in the dark when nobody could see, Alfie would take the cork out of the bottle; the fairy would do the work, and before dawn Alfie would put the fairy back into the bottle. The fairy was Alfie's to command until he released him or somebody else did. In a few weeks word got around about how well Alfie was doing because as the castle rose up above the trees, it could be seen from miles around. A young lad called Kevin, from another tribe, a poacher by trade, was stealthily about his business one night when he found himself quite by accident looking from out of the woods at the castle Alfie was building The sun was almost gone; it was gloomy, not quite dark, when Alfie loomed into sight. Crouching down, Kevin watched Alfie take the cork out of the bottle releasing a plume of white smoke that formed into what looked to him like a little leprechaun. He watched all night, mesmerized, and couldn't believe what he was seeing. The little leprechaun was doing all the heavy work. When dawn was near, Alfie put his little helper back into the bottle. Kevin went home to his poor parents empty-handed that night. He had watched Alfie so intently from dusk to dawn that he hadn't caught any rabbits for the family pot. The family went hungry that day.

The next night, having snared a couple of rabbits, Kevin went to spy on Alfie again. The routine was exactly as before. At night Alfie released the leprechaun from the bottle, and when dawn approached, he put him back into it. As the sun rose, Alfie sat down on a stone to survey his night's work. He set the bottle on the ground beside him. But something distracted him. He got up and ran to the back of the castle to investigate, leaving the wee bottle lying on the ground where he had set it. He didn't return right away; something had his attention. Kevin waited an hour or more, and still Alfie didn't appear. Then stealthily circling closer to the bottle until he was directly behind it, he took his chance, ran out, picked it up, and ran back into the whin bushes. He didn't stop running, with his rabbits and bottle in hand, until he was almost halfway home.

Resting under an oak tree, he took the cork out of the bottle, and out popped the leprechaun, only he wasn't a leprechaun; he was a Viking fairy. They sat looking at each other for a while before either of them spoke. The fairy broke the silence and told Alfie how he had ended up in the bottle and how he could be freed to go back to his family. Then Kevin told the fairy his story and how difficult it was for his poor parents to scrape out a decent living for themselves and him. When he had finished, the Viking fairy made him an offer. If Kevin would set him free, he would grant him three wishes. To set the fairy free, all Kevin had to say when the fairy was out of the bottle was, "You are free to go," and the fairy would be set free.

Kevin thought about the Viking Fairy's offer for a moment or two before shaking hands to seal the deal. His first wish was that when freed, the fairy would do no one any harm. The fairy smiled. His second wish was that the pains that plagued his father would leave him, never to return, and that he would always be fit for his work. The fairy nodded his head. Kevin's last wish was that his mother's cow would yield her bountiful supplies of the best full cream milk in the glen. The fairy, with his little face creased in smiles, noted that Kevin had asked nothing for himself. Kevin was about to set the fairy free when the fairy suggested that first they go to his home and see if at least two of his wishes had come true.

It wasn't far to Kevin's home. When they got there, his father was up and about, fit as a fiddle, raring to go. Kevin's mother was up to her elbows in creamy milk under the udder of her cow. There was much joy that day in Kevin's home. The fairy decided they would never be poor again, but he kept that to himself. Kevin spoke the words of freedom, and the fairy disappeared. In a Viking country far away, a young prince awoke from a deep sleep, and his family rejoiced.

Olderfleet Castle was never finished because Alfie couldn't find his lost Viking fairy. Freddie, agog spluttered, "What happened to Alfie?"

"Ah, sure, that's a story for another day, Son. Ask your grandfather tomorrow when you see him. He'll tell you all about that," Bob said, enjoying the very thought of that meeting of minds. "Fancy a big ice cream?" Bob shouted after Freddie as he ran off, a driftwood sword in hand to repel invading Vikings from Sandy Bay.

Tucking him into bed that night, Freddie said, "Dad, would you tell me that story again?" As he slipped onto the bed beside him, Bob knew he would have to be word perfect; otherwise, well you know what children are like about favorite stories—no alteration, no deviation. Bob didn't know who fell asleep first.

Marjorie woke him on her way to bed.

Where Imagination Found Wings

My uncle Robert called for me on Saturday mornings to go for a walk. I don't why. I never thought to ask. Perhaps it was because he didn't have a son. From my home in Mill Lane we sometimes walked along the narrow-gauge railway line past Kane's lower foundry to a big pool in the Inver River known locally as "the plum." I didn't know why it was called "the plum," and neither did my uncle. Sometimes he would bring his fishing tackle and try to teach me to fly fish for brown trout, but I wasn't very good at casting the line. Other times we would walk farther and harvest blackberries, hazelnuts, and wild garlic when in season.

One Saturday we didn't do our usual walk. I followed him out of Mill Lane onto Mill Street, up Mission Lane, along Ferris Lane past the Mission Hall with its proud plaque proclaiming that John Wesley had preached there, and turned right along Pound Street. I was only eight years old, but I knew this route well. I walked it four times a day on my way to and from school past Mulholland's butcher shop hugging the low stone wall to crest Fair Hill. I didn't ask where we were going; I knew my place, and I was a quiet child.

At Fair Hill, his back to the car park, he pointed upward and said, "Jimmy, that's where we're going today." That's when I noticed the two books clasped under his left arm. My eyes obediently followed his pointing finger to an acropolis crowned with an elegant Flemish bonded neatly pointed tall red brick building—a building I had blindly walked past four times a day for three years. Above the huge red door I read the words "The Carnegie Free Library 1905" in a cartouche formed by a mason's hand.

Holding his big plowman's hand, we crossed Victoria Road and climbed up the fourteen concrete steps ascending to a plateau before the entrance, where we paused and surveyed all that lay below us. Though only three feet tall, I felt like a giant; I could see over the roof of the town hall and far beyond. I was already in wonderland, and I had yet to make it into the building.

We crossed the threshold of the library into a surprisingly small ornate entrance hall. The terrazzo marbled floor, the hardwood wainscoted walls, and the tall fully glazed paneled double doors invited us inward. Inside proper, I looked around drinking it all in. We were in a huge reception area. The floor here was terrazzo marbled too but a different color, and the ceiling was reaching to the sky. I felt tiny, my giant experience of self a moment ago demolished. The entrance hall wainscoting continued but not in wood, in beautiful shining green tiles finished with a course of molded dado tiles three-quarter-way up the walls. I turned a full circle in awe taking it all in and saw a small woman with wild-looking hair standing behind a table watching me through steel-rimmed glasses perched on the end of her nose. My uncle approached her and presented his books. She acknowledged him; it was clear they knew each other. She took cards from the fly leaves of the books, noted something, and then put the cards into what I know now was a card cataloging bureau. I would when familiar with the nuances of library life spend hours thumbing through that book card catalog bureau. I would also come to understand that the library was a very private, quiet place for lovers of real literature that invited the willing silence of its users.

When the ritual book returning ceremony was complete, my uncle said to the lady, his big hand on my shoulder, "I've brought you a new member." Before I knew it, I was signed up, inducted, and given my library membership card and a guided tour of the library. I had become a full member of the Carnegie Free Library, able to choose books to take home and read. I couldn't believe it. The lady, although she looked stern, was anything but. She was very kind to me. I couldn't hide my excitement, and she knew it.

The library had two floors. The ground floor, as I recall, had three or four rooms subdivided by very tall bookshelves that seemed to me to stretch from floor to ceiling. Each book rack had at least eight bookshelves. I could only reach halfway up them, but there were wooden steps I could use to climb and reach higher. Health and safety had yet to be invented, but that was where the excitement lay in it—reaching, stretching, the uncertainty, the unearthing of something novel. The second floor was the same. It was accessed by way of an impressive staircase graced all the way in its climb upward by the green tile wainscoting. The upper floor basically was two large rooms divided into nooks and crannies and secret places by the tall enfolding bookshelves, creating the little monk-like cells. I loved those spaces. I felt safe, secure, sheltered. I could be my quiet self. Each floor and each room was a labyrinth with its own particular appeal. I was looking for a book one day in one of the book-rack-formed cells when the lady librarian in passing said, "You're browsing?" I had to find a dictionary to find out what browsing meant. I became an avid browser. I browsed away many of my teenage evenings in the Carnegie Free Library. Perhaps too many but never ever ill spent.

Occasional hexagonal tables and chairs were dotted around here and there for members to sit and read. Proper hardwood polished tables and high-backed chairs, from which my little legs dangled and joyfully swayed in rhythm with the thoughts flowing through my mind from what I was reading when I sat on them.

The library had very distinct smells—odors in polite circles. Old book fragrances, I called them, perfumed each cell I browsed with a distinct bouquet. If I was reading something about seafaring, I would experience the tangy smell of seawater, taste salt on my lips, and feel the sea breeze fanning my face. Reading poetry I could scent bluebells posing under trees or cheerfully respond to clouds of nodding daffodils. The hands that held the books and turned the pages before me added their characteristic flavors too. There really is nothing like the ever-lingering fragrances and textures of old rack-stacked outward-spine-facing books on seldom dusted shelves.

Daylight from the large windows that perforated the external walls of the library failed to adequately illuminate the book-racked cloistered cells, adding atmosphere and mystery. Artificial lighting added a cozy yellow glow. Often I followed the changing light around the library, book in hand, leaning on window shelves lost in a world of my imagination.

Each book borrowed was checked out by hand. The lady always at the desk had time for people; there was interaction. I learned to small-talk and enjoyed it. Sometimes queues formed while members checked out their two or three or half a dozen books. I secretly people-watched and discovered what they were reading; sometimes it surprised me, like the little old lady with her bundle of Mills and Boon. Perhaps she had never married, never known love, and maybe she was lonely. I would never know it was none of my business. I peeked inside their private worlds, one book cover at a time.

In the beginning using the card catalog was a bit overwhelming, but the lady at the desk was ever ready to help. Eventually I mastered it and enjoyed searching through the little drawers treasure hunting. There were so many subjects, titles, authors, and reference books that I spent many childish Saturday afternoons rooting through those drawers. Sometimes someone would misplace a card for the book I was looking for, but I never gave up the quest. The hunt was on. I was in hot pursuit. Imagine the triumphant feeling when the sought-after card was discovered and the much-sought-after book was in hand.

Books chosen, the process of manually—or womanly, should I say—checking them out was poetry in motion. I would walk up to the lady at the desk and present my books and cards. She would inspect everything to ensure all was in order; I would sign the cards, and she would date stamp them to complete the transaction. I loved the sound of the date stamp impressing on paper, the smell of ink, and the careful depositing of the cards in the little pouches inside on the covers. I did notice she took great care over her fingernails. She had her own fragrance too. Every day was a learning day for me in the library.

At home before I read any book I carefully examined the checkout card. It was the virtual life story of the book: when it was last checked out, who had read it before me, did I know them, did they pay any fines for late returns, and how long had it sat on the shelf before my little hand brought it back to life. But the thing I loved most of all was being rewarded, as it were, with a new, clean, crisp card. I would be first in the new history of this book for the readers following me for as long as the card had entry spaces vacant. The cards could take up to a dozen entries, so I could be top of the checkout list for quite a while. It was a great feeling.

The day when I became a member of the library, the first book I chose was *A Spotter's Guide to Birds*. The reason I chose it, I told my uncle, was that I wanted to learn how to identify all the birds we saw on our walks—and I did, book in hand, teach myself with my uncle by my side to identify them by their plumage, bird song, habitat, feeding preferences, flight patterns, and nests. I found where they nested, saw how they made their nests, and discovered the size, shape, colors, and patterns of their eggs before they hatched. I observed fledglings leave the safety of the nest for a bigger world just as I would grow up to do. I recorded all the birds I saw in a little book, which I still have to this day. Three birds I probably will never see again come to mind. One day we spotted a white blackbird! It's absolutely true; it had nested along the Inver River by Beach Green. Its mate was a genuine blackbird. The white one, my uncle said, was an albino. That was another word I had to look up in the dictionary. People came from miles around to see it. My uncle said they were twitchers—the people, not the birds. I spotted corncrakes and cuckoos before they sadly disappeared from our local landscapes. All this I got from the first book I borrowed from the Carnegie Free Library.

Other books followed, creating a trail—*Tom Brown's Schooldays*, *Huckleberry Finn*, *Robinson Crusoe*, *Treasure Island*, *A Tale of Two Cities*—and I was in them all: bullied at school, I found a solution; sailing down the river, later I would discover Rosa Parks and all she stood for; shipwrecked on an island, I learned how to survive; searching for treasure, I was Jim Hawkins to Long John Silver; and on the streets of London and Paris, I came face-to-face with resurrection men and revolution.

Then I discovered science, technology, engineering, languages, literature, and ambition. I discovered I had a future; it was up to me. As I savored these thoughts, my imagination sprouted wings; I could visit at will every land my imagination could find. What a feeling—what a joy to be free, to be curious.

In the cloistered cells of the Carnegie Free Library, my imagination found its wings. That is why without hesitation I can say it is my favorite place.

The Carnegie Free Library closed its doors as a library in 1980 to make way for a new library on Pound Street. The new library is good, but it's not the same. The bookshelves are supermarket shelves. It's open plan; there is little privacy. The furniture is plastic. People sit facing walls looking into screens. Books are checked in and out by machines. And it's impersonal, different.

Today the Carnegie Free Library building still proudly adorns its Acropolis, fulfilling its original educational function in different ways perhaps but just as effectively. It is the home of the Larne Museum and Arts Centre and vibrates daily with enthusiastic liveliness and energetic activity. Larne Art Club occupies one of the upper rooms to foster and encourage expression, interest, and participation in the visual arts by tutoring, training, demonstrating, and exhibiting members' works. The club meets weekly throughout the year. The other larger upper room is used by Larne Drama Circle to promote the performing arts by way of weekly readings of plays to which the public at large are encouraged to participate—workshops and an active program of outreach activities. It is the rehearsal and set building space for the Drama Circle's two annual public productions of contemporary thought-provoking dramas. Through the year the museum offers a diverse program of talks, lectures, exhibitions, and workshops that appeal to young and old in addition to the museum exhibits that inform us all of whom we are and where we are from.

The Carnegie Free Library was the place my imagination found wings.

L - #0283 - 181119 - C0 - 210/148/9 - PB - DID2679680